The
Raven's
Fall

The
Raven's
Fall

Emerald Raven Series

Book Two

ROSE WALKEN

The Write Moves Press

ISBN: 978-1-7362430-4-6 (hardcover)
ISBN: 978-1-7362430-3-9 (paperback)
ISBN: 978-1-7362430-5-3 (eBook)

Library of Congress Control Number: 2021916844

This book is a work of fiction. Names, places, characters, and incidents are the product of the author's imagination or are used fictitiously.

Book design by Will Silva

First edition 2021

The Write Moves Press
1123 MD RTE 3 North #264
Gambrills, MD 21054

1 2 3 4 5 6 7 8 9 10

For Damien and Lillian, my world

I want to thank those of you who read the first book and have returned to see if Tori and Mitch—*ahem* Logan—get the happily ever after they deserve.

If you are new to my books, I urge you to read the first installment of this series, The Raven's Call, first. Although there are references to some of the events of book one, I kept them to a minimum so as not to disrupt the natural flow of the story.

Happy reading!

Chapter One

───────────── ❧ ─────────────

Tori

S HIFTING IN THE COLD leather seat, I did my best to stabilize Sebastian's head against my shoulder. His light snores were comforting. I had to hand it to my son; he was a resilient five-year-old.

"Tori, do you want me to lay Sebastian down here—give your arm a rest?" The question came from the man I'd been trying hard to ignore for the past several hours, Professor Mitch Logan. Or whatever his name was.

Avoiding his gaze, I flicked my eyes toward the opposite side of the sleek limo that had met us outside the LAX tarmac several hours earlier. What they settled on gave little comfort.

Shaking my head in answer to Mitch's question, I locked eyes with the green-eyed brunette that bore a striking resemblance to the man seated across from her.

Ana, Mitch's sister. Her curious gaze was too similar to the one I was trying hard to avoid. I turned back to the tinted window and the dense forest zipping by.

My phone buzzed from my front pocket for the third time since our abrupt departure. Digging it out, I saw the expected name announced as a missed call. *Cami.*

Sometimes, it paid to have a best friend with a near-telepathic connection with me. This wasn't one of those times. Ignoring the call—I didn't know what to tell her at the moment—I placed the phone back into my pocket, trying not to disturb Sebastian. I could imagine Cami's response to *"Hi, don't worry, but I'm being taken to an unknown location somewhere between California and Utah. Oh yeah, and I'm not going to Brazil for the accounting internship because it never existed and neither does the 'accounting department head' that you were convinced would be the enduring love of my life."* I wasn't sure who would freak out more—her or her husband, Eric.

Wincing at the thoughts, I considered my previous experiences with love. One man confused about his sexual orientation—check. One with an unshakeable drug addiction—check, check. But this?

All I knew was that a few hours ago, I was heading to Brazil for what I thought was a simple accounting internship with an attractive escort (two, counting his friend), my neighbor, Liz, and her son, Drake. And now, I was in a limo, being trailed by the latter three people—two of whom I'd involved in something I couldn't even explain.

In fact, the only explanation I had received for the sudden flurry of activity that had erupted at LAX shortly before our flight was due for boarding, was that it was something I needed to "just trust him on."

Ironic considering the declaration had come from the mysterious professor at my university that I was positive, at this point, wasn't even a real professor. When it was followed by the violent apprehension of a stranger who just seconds before had been stroking my son's head, I wasn't sure "trusting him" was ever going to be a possibility.

Tears of frustration threatened to spill from eyes throbbing with pressure. I thought three years of abstinence would spare me from repeating this pattern of picking the wrong guy. The universe, at large, seems determined to show me differently.

"It's just over this hill," Ana said.

"Are you sure he won't be there?" Mitch asked, raking his hand through the wavy hair that was more displaced than I'd ever seen it. It gave him a younger, more innocent look.

Steeling my defenses against his vulnerability, I faked a yawn until it became a real one. My eyes shuttered as I rested my head against the cool window.

"No, he's closing out some big deal he's been working on for over a year now. Although, you're going to have to talk to him sometime. He is our dad."

"Hmph."

I took longer, slower breaths, hoping they'd continue.

"I'm grateful he came to your aid, Ana, but you're a thirty-five-year-old woman and this is the second time you've seen the asshole in person. I'm thirty-seven and still have yet to do so. I wouldn't hold your breath for a warm reunion between us."

The simmering anger in his tone was one I hadn't heard from him since he rescued me from an attack in a parking garage. Coupled with the ease I had just seen him take out two large nasty characters at the airport, it was chilling.

"Did you forget how much mom struggled after he walked out on her?" he continued. "I'm surprised you just let him back in your life like it all meant nothing."

"That's not fair."

She sounded pissed. I couldn't blame her; I didn't know their situation, but I recognized someone shooting under the belt when I heard it.

Another awkward silence hit the air-conditioned interior. My eyelids flickered as shadows and light danced across them. I opened them slightly, zeroing in on Ana as she lifted her hand in a fluttering motion.

"A-and this isn't the second time I've met him," Ana dropped the bombshell and then sat back as if bracing herself for an explosion.

Not even caring if I was caught, I opened my eyes wide and fixed them on Mitch's face. He was unnaturally still, and my heartbeat picked up in tempo.

His lids closed for a moment and his breath expelled in a loud exhale. Opening them, he turned to glance at Sebastian, and I lowered my lashes before his eyes reached mine.

"We'll talk about this *interesting* bit of information later. Now isn't the time, Ana," he said, resignation giving his words a defeated tone.

The limo slowed and pulled onto a gravel road. Sebastian's head slipped from my shoulder, and I was forced to abandon my headrest. His eyes sprung open.

"Mom? Weah aw we?"

4

Before I could answer, Mitch butted in, "Hey bud, we're near my dad's house. Is it OK if we stop in for a little visit?" His forced joviality grated on my frazzled nerves.

"Yeah! Shuwh! Does youw dad know how to battle mean guys, too?" Hero worship fairly burst from his tone.

"Well …" Mitch flashed a faint smile. "The thing is, Sebastian—"

"Our dad isn't home at the moment because he's protecting someone from bad guys right now, bud," Ana interjected.

"Wow, is he a ninja?" Sebastian's forehead rose in a solitary line.

"No, he runs a company that saves people from being hurt by anyone that gets really mad at them."

I looked to Mitch, confused at this rosy picture painted of a father he hadn't seemed impressed with.

Shooting Ana a thunderous scowl that was gone almost before it materialized, Mitch turned back to Sebastian. "I suspect my dad finds money more fun to collect than good-guy points. However, I'm sure he has something awesome in the house that a boy your age will love— maybe a pair of practice nunchuks."

"Woohoo! Mom can I use them, pleeeaz?"

"Maybe, bud."

We pulled down a narrow driveway and I could see an opening in the trees just ahead. A gasp escaped as we passed into the clearing.

A formidable fortress stood in unapologetic splendor from the side of a rocky hill. A large man-made lake softened the austerity of the modern lines of the house. I was used to the open windows that were prevalent in California and scarcely found in Maryland where I was born, but this? It was a nod to the architect that such a transparent house could also appear indestructible. Much of that was owed to the wide slabs of sleek stone which rose in tall columns and spanned across the bottom of the home.

Where do you even enter this monstrosity? My fascination was echoed by Sebastian as he leaned toward the window facing the house. His excitement overflowed. "Wow! It looks like a fohtwess! Is THIS youw daddy's house?!"

Mitch stared out the window, much more subdued and a hell of a lot less impressed than Sebastian and I were at the sight.

Tight-lipped but gamely trying to appease Sebastian's excitement, Mitch answered, "It is, buddy. But we aren't staying long, OK? I don't want you to get your hopes up too much." He glanced at me, so much misery in his green eyes that I had to look away.

My breath hitched. The shock and pain of betrayal warred with the sympathy his obvious suffering engendered, threatening my composure.

I had so many questions.

I just wasn't sure I wanted the answers.

Chapter Two

Mitch

THE AMOUNT OF JOY and despair someone could feel in one combined moment was something I had never considered before. At least, not until several hours ago when Ana had shown up at the same time my hopes of building a new life had crumbled into a convoluted mess. To be fair, things had been tangled before her reappearance. Now they were so snarled, it would likely take a lifetime more than I had to sort it all out.

Stepping out of the door as it swung open to reveal a giant of a man (on my father's payroll for more than greeting guests, from the look of him), I was struck anew by the magnificence of the property. *Looks like Dad has done well for himself, despite his faithless, black soul.*

"Welcome, Mr. Ravenschall," the giant said, his expression neutral. "I'm Viernan. I've been instructed to ensure that you and your guests receive the utmost care. Would you like a tour?"

Ignoring the sounds of impatience emitting from behind me, I shook my head. "I appreciate the welcome, Viernan. I'd like to postpone the tour. If you can just show us to our respective rooms, that would be sufficient for now."

"Of course, sir." He turned toward a pink-cheeked woman I hadn't noticed standing behind him. "Mrs. Hunt?"

"I'd be delighted!" the woman beamed, stepping out from Viernan's shadow. "You poor dears, you must be starving and in want of a good bath. I've had your rooms readied, if you'll just follow me."

I'm surprised by the matronly look of what I assumed was my father's housekeeper. She didn't fit into the playboy lifestyle I had always attributed to the man.

Mrs. Hunt's smile widened as her gaze settled upon Sebastian but faded again as the shrill voice of a child sounded from the doorway behind us.

"But Moomm, I'm hungry!" Drake stomped through the door, his mother's hand guiding him forward.

Liz searched the room until she found Tori. The worry behind her look deepened my guilt. *It was my fault they were all drawn into this mess. None of them had asked for this.*

As her gaze shifted to mine, I was the first to look away. I deserved her reproach but after spending the past few hours in tight quarters being speared by an identical expression, I needed to recharge.

Fortunately, the housekeeper stepped in. "Of course you are, my dear. My name is Mrs. Hunt, but you can call me Mrs. H. I'm here to make sure you don't waste away from hunger. And what is your name?"

Drake grabbed his mother's leg and peeked up shyly from underneath his dark lashes. "Drake. And this is my mommy!"

Eyes twinkling, Mrs. Hunt nodded her head. "I thought she might be. And does Mommy have a name?"

"Elizabeth," Liz answered, her arms wrapping protectively around Drake's shoulders. "My friends call me Liz." Her wary tone suggested she was holding back judgment of which category the housekeeper fell into. For now.

It was the first time I had heard steel in her tone. Not that I was surprised. Considering what she'd been hit with today, I admired her pluck.

"They are both beautiful names. You can call me Mrs. H, dearie. Well, Mr. Ravenschall didn't tell me we were to be delighted with *two* hungry, growing boys, but you aren't to worry yourselves a bit. Mrs. H will have you straightened out in a jiffy!" She walked over to an intercom on the suede-textured walls and pushed a button. "Ms. Lottie?"

"Yes, Mrs. H?" was the immediate reply.

"Please prepare the room adjoining Ms. McKinley and Mr. Sebastian's room, dearie. Oh, and tell Mr. Blasson that we'll need two more dinner services—one for a very hungry boy." Turning back to us, she gestured toward a doorway. "Follow me, please."

I could feel twin laser beams of outrage boring into my back as I followed the housekeeper through an impressive foyer and up a marble staircase that took up much of the entranceway.

I know, I know, Tori. I have some explaining to do. My mouth pulled to one side at the understatement.

Chapter Three

~

Tori

SITTING ON THE FOUR-POSTER bed in the middle of the biggest bedroom I had ever seen, I ran my hands across the stark-white duvet cover, marveling at the softness.

Sebastian's exuberant splashes sounding from the bathroom were comforting.

A knock from the connecting door heralded Liz's entry.

"Tori? Is it OK to talk?"

"Yes, Sebastian is washing up. I take it Drake is enjoying the mini-pool they call a bathtub around here?"

She nodded before sitting next to me. "It's all a bit overwhelming. But how are you dealing with all of this? W-with *him*? I know this can't be easy for you."

Marveling at the selfless wonder that was my friend, I shook my head. "No way am I letting *you* let *me* off the hook that easily. How are you doing? How is Drake? What did David have to say for himself? I'm so sorry, Liz. I should have—"

"It's not your fault, Tori. Drake and I are fine. D-david didn't shed any light on the situation. I was hoping you had learned something from your professor."

"Other than he's not likely a professor?" I scoffed. "The only thing I know is that the girl that was with him is his sister, Ana, and this is their father's house. Mitch said something about him not seeing his dad in a long time and he thought Ana hadn't either. That doesn't seem to be the case and Mitch wasn't happy to learn of it."

"What type of family can't even tell the truth about when they've seen each other?" Liz wondered aloud.

I shrugged and we fell silent while our son's sounds of delight could be heard from their respective bathtubs. *To have a child's capacity to be completely present in the moment.*

"Speaking of telling the truth," Liz began, her hands fidgeting in her lap. "I—uh—have something I need to tell you."

"What's wrong?"

Liz took a deep breath before everything escaped in a rush, "I grew up with David before he was David. I mean, we dated in high school, and he went by his first name, Sam, back then. I suspected at Sebastian's party, but I wasn't sure it was him until we were at the airport. It's been a decade since I have seen him. B-but I recognize his scent, the scar in his eyebrow that he got from falling off his bike when we were fourteen—oh!"

She cut off this fascinating news with a cry of dismay, burying her hands in the curtain of hair now covering her face. I was frozen in shock until I saw her shoulders shaking.

Leaning forward to wrap both arms around her, I squeezed gently while making soothing sounds. "Shh, it's OK." Rocking us back and forth, my mind was racing with thoughts of what this could mean. *Was all this based on Liz and not on me and Sebastian at all? Was Mitch just using me so David could get to her? Why? And if so, why had he acted like he hadn't seen their instant attraction when I brought it up to him? Why this elaborate ruse with offering me an accounting internship in another country?*

Each scenario made less sense than the next. One thing was certain, I needed answers. The not knowing was eating me alive.

Focusing back on the woman who was now sitting calmly inside my arms, I pulled back and tucked a section of black hair behind her ear. "Hold on, I'm going to go check on the boys and bring you some tissue. Stay right here."

"Thanks, Tori," she said quietly, wiping the moisture away from her reddened cheeks.

"You've got it." Sliding off the bed and walking toward the bathroom, I heard Sebastian's voice ring out, its pitch lowered into a proper villain's.

"You'll nevah catch me!"

Knocking on the door so as not to startle him, I waited for his "Yes, Mommy?" before opening the door. The sight filled my heart with joy. Sebastian was sitting in the middle of an enormous whirlpool tub surrounded in marble. A line of action figures was carefully perched on the rim while a couple more were being swirled through the air in his soapy hands. Iridescent bubbles topped the froths of white-capped water I had partially filled the tub with.

Where Mrs. H found the toys and bubble bath was a mystery, but they all looked new. It seemed she was expecting us. This evidence of the lies we had been living threatened the genuine happiness that seeing Sebastian's joy had caused. Snapping out of it, I smiled down at my son, reaching into the water to make sure the temperature was still warm.

"You have a few more minutes to play before I come in to help you wash, bud. I'm right outside the door, talking with Ms. Liz if you need me."

Stepping out of the bathroom, I handed Liz the tissues I had grabbed and crossed the room to enter her and Drake's room. I noticed our rooms were almost identical.

She had the same four-poster bed covered in white linens and eclectic mix of modern, minimalistic tables flanked by chunkier chairs. The artwork hanging over her simple writing desk was a landscape done in vibrant blues and greens, while mine contained splashes of crimson and vibrant orange. Her window was larger than the one in my room and the sheer curtains were drawn back to let the breathtaking lakeview take center stage. *Whatever Mitch's Dad's faults may be, lack of taste is not one of them.*

The thought gave me the boost I needed as I rapped on the partially open bathroom door. "Hey, Drake! Your mom and I are talking in my room. I'm just grabbing something for her. She wanted to know if you were ready to get out yet?"

"No, thanks!" was the expected reply. More splashing punctuated his response and I smiled as I heard him doing similar voices to what

Sebastian had been using. Mrs. H must have split the toys. Or, Liz had packed their own.

"OK we have the door open so we can hear you if you need anything. Your mom will be coming in a few moments to help you wash up and dry off."

"OK!"

Walking back into my room, I found Liz at the window. One side of the curtains had been drawn back and she was staring out at the shimmering lake.

"Hey, you alright?"

She started. "Yes, sorry. Just thinking about the last time I spoke with David in high school."

Her mouth turned down as her hand clenched around the tissue. "Not a pleasant event, I'm guessing."

"No, it wasn't," she breathed, turning toward me with a fractured smile. "In fact, it—

A knock interrupted whatever she was going to say.

Locking eyes with Liz, I shrugged and answered, "Yes?"

"Ma'am, it's me, Miss Lottie, with your dinner trays. May I come in?"

My stomach grumbled in answer. "Yes, please come in."

A young woman with a head full of tawny curls pinned in artful disarray entered the room, pushing a cart laden with covered dishes. A cacophony of spices blended together in a savory bouquet that had my nose rising to take it all in.

"That smells delicious!" Liz and I laughed as we voiced our approval in unison.

15

"Pardon me, ma'am's, but Mr. Blasson—he's Mr. Ravenshall's cook—is known as the best chef this side of the North Fork Mokelumne River. Why, Viernan and I always say—Oh! Forgive my running on," she said, the pink in her cheeks making her rosebud mouth stand out even more. "Still, I'm certain he'll be right pleased to hear of your approval!" Her beaming smile revealed a gap between her two front teeth, adding to her unique charm.

"Well, if it tastes as good as it smells, I think we are fortunate to get this chance to sample his art," I responded, returning her smile.

Turning my head, Liz and I locked eyes, the hunger from the past few hours spent without sustenance causing a pinched look on her face that was surely echoed on my own.

"Well, Miss Lottie, is it? Thank you so much for bringing us our meals. I think we can handle things from here. We need to get the boys cleaned up if we have any hope of enjoying our meals while they are warm," I laughed.

"Oh, I have two young ones at home. I understand exactly what you mean!" Leaning down, Lottie pulled something out from the bottom of the cart and snapped it open, revealing a standing food tray. "These will make it a little easier for you and the boys, rather than trying to balance a plate on your laps. If you need me or Mrs. H, just push the green intercom button and then the numbers '0' and '3'. We'll be happy to help." And with a nod of her curls, she exited the room as suddenly as she had entered it.

As the door clicked shut, Liz turned back to me with a smile. "She is extremely sweet. And oh my, this food!"

"I agree on both counts. As much as I want to hear the rest of your story, Liz, I'm going to suggest we continue this conversation after the boys go to bed. I'm famished. Maybe we can let them sleep in your room tonight while we talk in mine."

"That sounds perfect. I'll meet you back here in a few minutes." She took one last look at the dinner cart before disappearing through the connecting door.

Walking toward the bathroom and hearing Sebastian's boisterous play, I wondered how much of a fight I was about to receive. Without the level of fuel I was used to having before dealing with bath time protests, I wasn't looking forward to it.

***

Rubbing the stomach testing the stretching power of my waistband, I threw my head back in contentment. "I wish Cami could have tasted that. Although, she would have immediately demanded the recipes from Mr. Blasson."

"I'm not sure a chef of his caliber would be willing to give them to her," Liz smiled.

"We're talking about Cami. I don't think he would have had a choice."

"Ha! Very true. She can be—a bit persuasive," she said, worrying her lip.

"It's OK, Liz, I know you told her what's going on."

"I'm so sorry, Tori! She threatened to report you as a missing person if I didn't tell her where you were!" Her voice was hushed so as not to disturb the boys watching TV from the end of the bed.

She needn't worry. *The Last Jedi* was playing on one of the hundreds of available channels. Now that their initial hunger has been sated, the boys were devoting all their attention to the screen.

Chuckling, I reached out a hand to cup her arm gently. "Don't worry about it. I know how determined Cami is when she wants something. You didn't stand a chance."

Her shoulders relaxing, she nodded. "It only takes a person a few moments to figure out why she's so successful. Still, I knew she was worried about you and if the situation were reversed, I would want to know."

"You're right. And if I wasn't such a coward, you wouldn't have been in that position to begin with. I just don't have any answers to give her," I sighed. My head had lost some of the fogginess that had enveloped it as soon as violence erupted at the airport. "And I think it's about time that I got some. Liz, would you be alright staying here with the boys while I find out what's going on?"

"Of course! Take your phone and promise me you'll call if you need help, Tori."

The concern on her face broke through my single-mindedness. I gave her hand a squeeze after letting Sebastian know I'd be gone for a little while. "It's not me who will be calling out for help, I can assure you of that."

Her chuckle followed me out the door.

Chapter Four

Mitch

"VIERNAN, I'D LIKE THAT tour now. You can end with whatever version of a gentleman's lounge my father has in this house. This young pup here has a sudden wish to get schooled in billiards."

David snorted as Viernan cracked a smile before answering. "Yes, Mr. Ravenschall. Your father has converted the entire lower level into just such a space. He keeps an excellent port there, too, if I may add."

"Hopefully, he keeps some tissues for all the tears this old man is about to shed when I hand him his balls," David taunted, slapping me on the back.

Not deigning to respond, I let an eyeroll display my opinion of his trash talking and nodded to Viernan to begin. In truth, David was one of the best 9-ball players I'd ever met. I was looking forward to the concentration needed to best him.

"This way, sirs. We'll start with the great room since you've already seen the front entrance. It adjoins Mr. Ravenschall's study, where he has an impressive collection of books, if anyone in your party is an avid reader."

My thoughts immediately jumped to a certain temptress who was probably thinking of a hundred ways to skewer me. Wondering if Tori enjoyed reading wasn't helping, though, so I answered with a noncommittal grunt. The sight enfolding before me as I walked through a curved archway provided an easy distraction.

David's low whistle echoed my thoughts.

"Man, I thought you told me you grew up in a small house. If this is your idea of small…"

"I did. As did Ana. I told you, we lived with my mother. This is the first time I've stepped foot in my father's house." Holding his gaze for a moment, I turned back to Viernan, who was standing in the middle of the room. The fact that this giant of a man barely registered among the other items in the room was a testament to the enormity of vertical space it offered.

"The ceilings are thirty feet tall. The wall of windows behind me are fixed with several layers of bulletproof glass, as are all the windows in the house. With a flick of a switch, they can be set to a mirrored reflection which allows anyone inside to see what, or whom, is outside, while making sure nothing can be seen inside." Moving toward one of two fireplaces in the room, he gestured for us to move in closer.

David and I drew nearer, like two kids being enticed into a magic show.

"I want to show you this, sirs, out of an abundance of caution," Viernan stated, his tone deepening. "With the two young ones soon roaming about, Mr. Ravenschall thought it best to apprise you of all potential dangers. This is certainly not your average home," he said, raising an eyebrow.

Contorting his limbs into a kneeling position in front of the dark fireplace, he reached an arm inside and held his hand in front of the side wall. A distinctly metallic clang sounded from inside the hollowed wall sending a jolt of adrenaline coursing through me. A glance at David showed a similar reaction. He turned briefly toward me before fixing his gaze back on the fireplace opening.

"My apologies for the unexpected nature of this particular security measure, but it was designed for that very purpose...to surprise anyone foolish enough to try an unorthodox manner to enter the home. With the warm temperatures here, it would be rightly deduced that the fireplace would not be used often, and therefore could prove a temptation for any unsavory sort wanting to use it as an entrance. Mr. Ravenschall has installed retracting steel spikes to be activated either by a motion sensor located several feet above this panel, or by here, with a fingerprint reader that only a few of us are programmed into."

I was impressed by the ingenuity, despite my best efforts. Beside me, David chuckled.

"I guess that would take care of any stray vermin problems, too, huh?"

Viernan's lips twitched. "Yes, sir." He turned toward a pair of massive doors at the back of the room. "And this is where Mr. Ravenschall's study is, if you'll follow me."

An uneasy feeling hit me as I followed Viernan. I had hoped to set Tori and Liz's minds at ease after the shock of violence they had seen at the airport, but with new dangers added, it seemed futile. Sighing, I stopped a couple of feet from where Viernan was gesturing toward the study doors.

"These doors can withstand hurricane winds to bullets, to minor explosions and fire. This room was originally meant to be a safe room, but Mr. Ravenschall decided to go one step further, as you will soon see." And with that, he threw both doors open, stepping back to allow us entry.

The first thing I noticed as I entered was the ornately carved desk. Discomfort at finding something my father and I had similar tastes on gave way to an appreciation of the intricate details.

From here it looked like the work of a master craftsman.

"Phew!" David's whistle snapped my head back. "You weren't kidding when you said he has a lot of books. It must have taken a while to build a collection of this size!"

Only then did I notice the thousands of books lining the walls.

"A lifetime, actually."

I froze. Although I had never heard his voice this close, there was no mistaking the unique rasp I'd caught from his media appearances.

"Mr. Ravenschall! We didn't expect you back so early. Welcome home, sir!"

"Thank you, Viernan. It feels good to be home. I see we have some company. Son, it's good to see you."

David's shock was comical, and I leaned toward him. "Close your mouth, you'll just feed the bastard's ego."

"You never told me your father was the CEO of LARS Security!" he hissed.

I gave him a curt nod before turning to set eyes on a man that I had never seen outside of a TV screen or media publication. "Ana tells me I have you to thank for extracting her and Justin from Brazil. She asked if I could express my appreciation in person, so here I am. Thank you. Now, if you'll excuse me." And with that, I turned toward the door with barely a glance at a still gawking David.

A choked off laugh barked from behind me before I felt the grip of a firm hand. "Please, don't go yet."

I turned my head and glanced down at the hand still grasping my shoulder before meeting my father's blue-green eyes. They were more bloodshot than in the magazine photos, the irises less bright. But they were still the same unique color that had captivated my mother when she had met the hotshot Marine in her twenties. "I wish you and Ana had taken on your father's eye color," she had lamented more than once. "They were like sea glass. I always felt like he had an otherworldly look about him. It was a big part of his appeal. Not just to me, but to all the ladies…young or old." It was here she would stop, seeming to snap out of a sadness that made me hate him more each time. She never came out and said he had been unfaithful, but I was able to put the pieces together. The fact that she never spoke of him with anger clouding her tone was testament to how big a grip he had had on her giving heart. I didn't think she ever stopped loving him. And he had walked out on her, twice, without a backward glance.

Allowing years of contempt free rein on my face, I looked back at his hand before meeting his gaze without flinching. I got a moment of satisfaction as he jerked it back, his smile faltering.

"I think we've said everything that needs to be said." Shoulders held stiffly back, I walked toward the doors, not sparing a glance at David.

"That's where you're wrong, Logan. I'm afraid I've got some very important information regarding the safety of a few people under your protection."

This stopped me in my tracks, as I was sure he intended.

David cursed before moving deftly to the side of me.

I was relieved to see his loyalty overcame whatever hero worship he felt for my father. I sent him a nod before turning around to face my father once more.

"First, 'Logan' does not exist for another couple of months. You can address me as Raven or, until I've been given the official word that this assignment has been completed, Mitch. Second, what information do you think you're privy to that my agency is not?"

"Victoria McKinley, Elizabeth Sonneman, and their children are in grave danger. Even if you wanted to, you cannot return them to their former residences," he stated matter-of-factly.

Relieved, I chuckled. "Thanks, but we've already deduced that. Why the hell do you think I was taking them to Brazil to begin with? We planned on letting the team get the information from Mikaela and her father about any other threats before returning the women and kids back to their homes. So, I'm afraid your important information is actually old news."

"Logan, you've been misinformed. I don't mean they can't be returned to their homes now. I mean not ever."

A gasp sounded from behind and I closed my eyes briefly, already guessing whom I would find there. Opening them and turning slowly around, I caught sight of Tori McKinley, her full lips parted.

Snapping her mouth closed, she speared my father with a thunderous look. "Just what the hell do you mean by that? I want to go home. My son wants to go home!" Swinging to me with bright eyes sparking in fury, she asked, "What did you get us into? What does he mean, *Logan*, by we can't be returned to our homes…ever?"

Letting out a deep breath, I raked my fingers through my hair. "Tori, I'm sure it is something that we can fix—just let me—"

"No, son," my father interjected. "This is much bigger than you know. None of you will be safe there for a very long time. It's time to formulate a new plan. And I can help you, if you let me."

"No. Tell me what you know, and David and I will figure this out."

I was studied for several seconds before he sighed. "I'll tell you, but I mean what I said. If you let me help you, I can make things a lot more comfortable for you. This is what I've built an entire empire on. Keeping people safe when the world wants to harm them. You can trust me, son."

"Like you kept mom safe?" His flinch was satisfying. "No thanks, I'll take my chances with the people I can actually count on. David, escort Tori into the great room. Mr. Ravenschall and I have a few things to discuss."

"Sure. Tori?" David looked to Tori as he swung an arm toward the doors.

She didn't move. Her eyes were steady on mine even as the redness along her cheeks spread to her chest. "I'm not going anywhere until I get some answers. What did he mean by saying we can't ever go back home?"

"Tori, please. Trust me." I knew I didn't have a right to ask it, but the words slipped out before I could give them much thought.

Something flickered across her features. "I did. And you lied to my face and put my loved ones in danger. Now I want to know how you're going to fix it."

She had never been as beautiful to me as she was in that moment. Whether she realized it or not, she just revealed she still entrusted me with the safety of her and her loved ones. A feigned cough from my father broke the hold this unexpected gift had me wrapped in.

"I understand, Tori," I told her, my eyes never wavering from hers. "And I will tell you as much as I can, shortly. However, there are bigger stakes here and if I don't get all the information I need, I could be putting even more lives at risk. This shouldn't take longer than fifteen- to twenty-minutes." I received my father's nod of acknowledgment before turning back to her. "And I will fill you and David in together, directly after."

She bit down on the bottom lip that I might never taste again. "Fine. If you take any longer, I'm coming in whether you two want me there or not. I've waited long enough."

And with that, she glided through the doors with her chin held high.

David sent a lopsided grin before he turned toward the doorway. He was stopped short as Ana sauntered into the room.

"You boys didn't think you were having this little family reunion without me, did you?" The minx grinned before sitting in one of the two chairs facing the desk.

I waited until David closed the heavy doors behind him and Tori before I took a seat next to my sister. We both turned to look at the man we grew up swearing we'd never let into our lives.

"Your meeting, I believe, Father."

"Right." Sighing, he sat down behind the desk, his fingers drumming across the inlaid border. "I guess I should start from the very beginning."

"That would most likely be the best place," Ana drawled and my mouth twitched. The past six months of her disappearance were starting to feel like the moment you woke from a nightmare and realized you were still safely in the midst of reality.

"Of course. Then I'll just get right into it," my father said, shifting. "Your mother wasn't a social worker when I met her."

This caused only a mild interest. I knew my mother had met my father when she was twenty-two, a time when many young adults were still figuring out what they wanted their summer job to be rather than their careers.

"Where did she work, then?" Ana asked, smiling. "Wait, don't tell me. She was a flight attendant? Or maybe a magician's assistant?" she scoffed. "No offense, Dad, but what does Mom's career path have to do with me spending six months in a safehouse deep in the wilds of Brazil?"

"Or with Christoff and Mikaela Blanc?" I chimed in.

"Much more than you two could ever imagine," he sighed, the ridges etched into his forehead deepening. "Your mother and I were always supposed to tell you this together. Looks like you got out of this one too, Evie," he said into the empty space above.

The affection in his tone was unsettling.

Ana blew out an inpatient breath. "Dad, we're all adults here. Spill it."

His smile softened the rugged jaw as his eyes took on a faraway look. "Your mother was one of the best damn field officers the CIA had at the time. And I was fortunate enough to be on the tech support team for quite a few of her assignments."

The confession hung in the air as thick and stagnant as the sludge in a forgotten pond.

Mom worked for the agency?

I recovered my voice first. "How did she end up a social worker then?"

"She became pregnant with you, Logan. And all that mattered to her from that moment on was making sure you kids were safe. She changed her name, her appearance, and of course, her career. We both thought that would be enough. Hell, we even demanded the agency keep an eye on us that first year after she left and you were born. When nothing happened, no one showed up on our doorstep, we got complacent. You don't know how much I wish I could go back to that time."

I was reeling from the raw pain and regret seeping out of a man I had spent my life vilifying. Then I realized none of this exonerated him from walking out on us. If anything, it made his disappearance even more reprehensible since he left us all exposed to God knows what. Forcing a civil tone, I prodded, "You grew complacent and then...?"

"When you were ten months old, I came back from assignment in Brazil. We had received word about a sex ring that someone with business ties in the U.S. was running. They were supplying a steady stream of girls, some as young as twelve years old, as gifts to the elites. Corporate directors and CEO's, celebrities and their agents, and members of some of the most respected 'old money' families were all being investigated. Hell, the agency was coordinating with ten other agencies from four countries. I must have set up taps and infiltrated the networks of a few dozen of the world's largest corporations. It was going to be the biggest takedown of our time," he said with pride before sighing. "Then we got a lead that changed everything. One of our agents acquired a list of U.S. government officials—heavily encoded, of course—that had made payments to the shell company that was at the heart of the sex ring." A muscle pulsed in the side of jaw as he continued, "Several of our embassies, national security departments...all the way to the top of the food chain, were involved."

He grew silent, and I was grateful for the reprieve.

Ana sat motionless beside me. We had both been in this business long enough to understand the far-reaching consequences of such a discovery. The stonewalling, evidence destruction, and untimely disappearances of key players were just some of the challenges those in our line of work must contend with. Of course, there were times when we assisted in these activities. It always came down to the greater good...for someone.

"What we didn't consider was the price for that list. Not until the people involved in the investigation started turning up dead. Hell, not just them; anyone unlucky enough to be around when the reaper came calling." His voice softened. "I lost a good friend and longtime agent. And before he lost his life, he watched them gun down his wife and three-month-old little girl."

"I'm so sorry, Dad. You think it was a swap?" Ana asked.

"Yes. We questioned our agent and discovered he had received the first list from someone who claimed to be with the FBI. When we spoke with them, we learned there was only a handful of people that could have had access to where that information had been stashed. They initiated a lockdown and investigation that morning that ended in IDing the most likely perpetrator. We took care of the rest. He was surprisingly easy to break."

"I take it some of our guys in the embassy were a part of this ring?" I asked, although I was fairly certain of the answer.

"Quite a few of them," he confirmed. "And when the list of names came out, it had the names we were using on current assignments. I knew it was just a matter of time before they caught up to me. The risks were just too great. So, I convinced your mother to move again, this time without me. And to make sure you kids wouldn't ask too many questions later, I made your mother swear to cast me as just another absentee father. So, if you think I blame you for the contempt in your eyes or resentment in your tone, you're wrong. It's only what I deserve."

"Oh, Dad!" Ana jumped up and sprinted around the desk to where our father was already rising from his chair.

"For all of these years—I—we—" she warbled into his shoulder.

I stared at the two of them, my mind churning with questions. "What made you think coming back around a year later was a good idea? How was getting Mom pregnant again supposed to protect us?"

I almost missed the quick pinching in his face as he pulled out of Ana's embrace. "You're right. I tried to tell her the same thing when she showed up at my flat that night with you clutching tightly to her hand. But she was so beautiful," he sighed. "And seeing you—my baby boy—after so long…" His face got steely as he reached for Ana's hand. "Besides, I don't regret that night one bit. It gave me this beautiful, strong woman as a daughter."

Ana smiled at him through her tears, lightly swinging their connected hands.

For the first time since walking into his study, I fixated on the thousands of books lining the walls.

"So, she became a social worker, living the extremely modest lifestyle of a single parent while you built one of the largest security companies in the United States. Seems a bit of a lopsided plan, to me."

"She chose her profession, Logan," he said, letting go of Ana's hand. He waited until she was seated again to continue. "And no matter how it looked to you, she always had enough money for whatever you needed. I made sure of that."

"It's too bad you couldn't provide her with the same level of security you've become an expert at offering others."

He stilled before exhaling. "You don't know how right you are. I'd do anything to have her here now. With the resources I have at my disposal, maybe I wouldn't have to face the next few decades without her."

Closing my eyes to this new pain, I willed myself to keep calm. "So, her death was no accident, I take it?"

"No."

My hands started shaking and I gripped the chair, wondering if Ana's silence meant she was as affected by this development as I was. I turned my head slowly toward her and saw her eyes pinned to my father's face, the muscle in her jaw pulsating. Her mouth opened but whatever she was about to say to him was cut off by a knock.

Mrs. H and a younger woman entered after my father's terse "come in", bringing a food cart.

"Excuse us, Mr. Ravenschall, we thought everyone could use some refreshments," she said cheerily. "Ms. McKinley and young Mr. Ravenschall's friend are enjoying a bite, as well."

"Thank you, Mrs. Hunt, Lottie. You can leave it here. I will serve our guests."

After one curious look from the woman he identified as Lottie, she and Mrs. H scurried from the room, leaving a heavy silence in their wake.

My father sprung to action, filling venetian-themed plates with fruit and baked treats before handing one to each of us. His blitheness grated as he expounded on his chef's culinary accomplishments. Ana did her best to match his tone, but her replies grew increasingly brittle.

I felt my control slip.

"Yes, your chef is obviously talented. Now why don't you cut through the bullshit and tell us how our mother really died?" I ignored Ana's sharp intake of breath as my father set his glass down with a snap.

"You're right. You two have waited long enough. The morning your mother got into an accident, she thought she was on her way to rescue me. She had received a package that contained a note and a lock of my hair. The note directed her to come alone to a remote location just outside of Fresno or they would start sending other parts of me that weren't as—renewable—I believe they called it."

"Do you know what they wanted?"

"Revenge. And they got it," he said softly. "She was ambushed on an open stretch of road. They found her twenty feet away from the wreckage, where she had been ejected through the windshield. The lock of hair—which wasn't mine—lie clenched in her hand."

Ana's fingers fluttered up to her face. The image warped as if viewed from the lens of a wide-angle camera.

I shook my head and my vision cleared.

"They found a letter on her?"

"No, the bastards mailed it to headquarters the day after your mother was buried. It had her bloody fingerprints on it," my father said, his shoulders sagging.

"Sounds too sloppy for a professional," I mulled. "First, a lock of hair that could easily provide traceable DNA, and then a letter that contained the same?"

"And to our agency? They had to have known forensics would have found something," Ana scoffed.

"Yes, we thought the same thing. And you are right, forensics did find something. Although, the processes weren't quite as advanced back then. The note was clean. The hair, however, …"

"Please tell me you nailed them." My jaw ached from the effort to keep it unclenched.

"We were able to identify the owner of the hair. It did not, however, lead to the apprehension of the man who sent it."

"Then whose was it? Some poor dead souls?" I asked. My thoughts were on a nauseating cycle as I realized my mother had died clutching the hair of a stranger. I hoped she had found comfort from it in those last moments.

My father shifted, leaning forward. "No, son. It was yours."

Chapter Five

———————— ❧ ————————

Tori

FINISHING THE BLUEBERRY MUFFIN that tasted as if it were made by the God of Baking himself, I glanced up at David. "So, his name is Logan and his father is the head of a security company."

"*The* security company. The one most of the developed world trusts with their clandestine operations. LARS Security does everything from protecting visiting foreign dignitaries to assisting in hostage recovery. Of course, most of that isn't generally known to the public, even though Mr. Ravenschall keeps a more public image than many of our contracted friends do. I still can't believe he's Raven's father."

"Yes, I've seen him in the commercials. I always thought they did home security."

"Oh, they do. Speaking of which, Viernan just showed us something you and Miss Harris need to know for the safety of the boys."

And with that fascinating pronouncement, David walked over to one of two fireplaces in the massive room. "These are equipped with a security feature that is triggered from below, here," he said, pointing to a small panel on the inside of the fireplace, "and from motion sensors inside the chimney above. When they are activated, spikes emerge from the walls inside, becoming both a weapon and an entryway obstruction."

I let out a breath and walked closer to the hearth. Bending down, I peered at the panel. "So, this is a motion sensor? Wouldn't that make it difficult to actually start a fire, if it were needed?" I asked in confusion.

Laughing, David answered, "You're right, of course. Only, this panel is a fingerprint reader. Viernan says there are just a few people programmed into the system. My concern is if the boys decided to climb upward from inside while a bird were to travel downward..."

The horrifying picture had me shaking my head. "Right, I got it. Thank you for telling me. I'll make sure Liz knows, too."

His look of relief struck me as excessive, although I knew he was fond of Sebastian. Then Liz's earlier words hit me and I realized who his concern was really for.

"Speaking of Liz, I heard the two of you have known each other since high school."

David turned abruptly to face the large windows. "Yes, we have. How long have you and Liz been friends?"

"Less than a year. I also heard that you were dating for a time." If he thinks I was going to be distracted by such an obvious dodge, he was mistaken.

"Right again. And then she met her future husband. Did she tell you about him? A decent guy and well-liked at school. I was sorry to hear about his death."

"Yes, I was too, although I never met him. Liz has always spoken very highly of him."

We grew silent, and I thought about our conversation before Mrs. H and Lottie had shown up with the serving cart. I had wasted little time in grilling David after the study doors had closed. No matter how much I demanded, he refused to tell me why or how I became involved in this mess.

Sighing, I had walked over to the same window he was now in front of, and watched the birds flying over the sparkling water. The night sky darkened until even the closest trees became shadows.

David's voice had cut in, "You can trust him, you know. He'll keep you safe. There isn't anyone who is ever worked with Raven that would tell you differently."

I spun around. "Safe from what, exactly? Whatever dangers *he* exposed us to, David? Is it somehow lost on either of you that my five-year-old son is now in danger and I don't even know how—or what—to protect him from?" I inhaled deeply through my nose before letting out the air that had grown cold in my chest.

"You're right. I'm sorry. My mom was the fiercest protector I ever had, too," he had stated softly.

The stillness of his features told me he was far away, but it was the yearning in his tone that had driven away the last of my anger. "Your mother passed?"

"Quite some time ago. It changed my world."

The simplicity of his answer struck me again as my mind returned to our present silence. I was surprised by how comfortable it felt.

With an energetic step, David walked over to a section of swords arranged on one wall. He whistled. "I've never seen beauties like these outside the pages of a book."

"Like the book you're writing?" I couldn't help but rib. Seeing his smile fade, I continued, "So, you're into swords?"

"All weapons, actually," he answered, his grin returning. "But these were made a long time ago. Look at the intricate design on the steel. It's a wonder when you consider the differences in technology between now and the 14th century, when this was likely made."

"You have an excellent eye, David," Mr. Ravenschall said from behind us.

I spun around to face the now open double doors of the study, Ana trailing behind her father while Mitch brought up the rear. Mitch's face looked set in stone, and my stomach fluttered.

While David and Mr. Ravenschall talked about the swords, Ana walked up to me, her face more open than it had been in the long car ride here. "Hi, Tori. I'm so sorry we had to meet under these circumstances. Although, if you hope to make it in this family, it's probably best to get everything out in the open now." Her mouth turned up on one side as she nodded her head toward Mitch, who was watching us from a few feet away. "We aren't the easiest group to love, no matter how pretty some of us were lucky enough to be born."

As I watched her eyes sparkle with contained laughter, I noted that pretty was an understatement when it came to her. She was breathtaking. The same combination of dark hair and vibrant green eyes she shared with her brother took on a seductive aspect when paired with a smooth complexion and softer, feminine features.

"Ana," Mitch cut in. "I doubt Tori cares about any of that at the moment." His eyes locked on mine and a sadness hit me so hard I was forced to look away. He was right. The time spent longing for a man who employed every waking moment lying had ended. All I cared about now was the safety of my loved ones.

"We can agree on that one thing, at least."

His eyes shuttered as he nodded, stepping back and gesturing toward the study. "It's about time I gave you some answers. Please, after you, Ms. McKinley."

Chapter Six

―― ❧ ――

Mitch

WATCHING TORI'S HAIR SWAY with her hips as she walked toward my father's study, I tried to summon the focus I'd need for the difficult discussion to come. In vain, of course. My fingers curled into my palms as they ached to wrap themselves around those hips.

"David," I snapped, interrupting his conversation with my father. "It's time."

"Thank you for the insight into your collection, Mr. Ravenschall. I'm in awe, to be completely honest, sir," I heard him say.

My father's answer was lost as I entered through the double doors, zeroing in on the occupant of the desk. Tori's back was ramrod straight, hovering a few inches from the chair. Wanting a clear view of her face, I took the seat my father had occupied.

Her hazel eyes met mine for an instant before landing on a spot just past my right ear.

David walked in, closing the doors softly behind him. "Say what you want, Raven, but your old man knows his weapons."

"Yes, well, I guess that isn't surprising since he spent decades wielding them."

David looked sharply at me before taking the empty chair next to Tori.

Sighing, I voiced aloud what my mind still wasn't comfortable facing, "It seems I've been misled about my father. And my mother."

I could feel Tori's curiosity but focused on David first. "I know you have questions, but I need to get Tori up to speed with what you know first."

He nodded, rising from his chair before stating, "Sure thing. I'll be over here looking at some reference books on Middle Age weaponry. I might have found a new calling. Let me know when you're ready for me."

Tori licked her bottom lip, drawing my attention. It took a moment to realize the silence had become an uncomfortable one.

Clearing my throat, I said the words I never thought to say, especially on the eve of my retirement. "My name is Logan Ravenschall. I work for the CIA, and when I met you, I had already read a file that gave me most of your life history. In fact, you were one of ten possibilities that the agency gave me to take along on Ana's rescue mission. She also works for the CIA."

The only sound in the room was the occasional page being turned as David did his best to appear engrossed in a book.

I watched in fascination as Tori's eyes first widened and then narrowed until they were mere slits. I was certain that if I had chosen the chair next to her, I'd now be nursing either a burning cheek or an aching jaw. Running a cursory scan of the objects in arms reach of her, I sighed in relief. Other than a pen and a few papers my father had pushed aside, there was nothing on the desk that posed an immediate threat.

"Is Ana even your sister?" she spit out.

"Yes, she is my sister, and Duke Ravenschall is my father. This is his house, and everything I told you about my family is true. Was true," I corrected. "Ana and I have just discovered that the details of our parents are not what we grew up believing. In fact, that is part of what I need to share with you as it is connected to how you and I met and why we are all in danger now. A danger I intend on eliminating as quickly as I can, Tori, I promise you."

"How did your agency even get my name? How was I chosen out of hundreds of thousands of kids within the university?"

"We received your name from someone who has a vested interest in the success of the rescue mission. Someone who happens to be one of your professors, and an admiring one, at that." I watched her closely, knowing from experience how quickly Tori could descend into shock.

"Not too admiring if she or he was willing to put me and my son through something like this." The accusation in her tone was unmistakable.

"Tori, I never would have let you or Sebastian come to harm."

"Oh really? Then why can't we go back home, Mit—damn it! I don't even know what to call you!"

Tears gathered in her eyes, and without another thought, I moved around the desk to take the chair next to her. Breathing in her scent, I took her trembling hands in mine.

"As much as I'd like to hear my name roll across your sweet lips, it's best if you continue calling me Mitch. This mission isn't over, even though Ana and Justin have been recovered."

"Who's Justin?"

"Justin is Ana's boyfriend. He accompanied her on assignment to Brazil to give her cover story some authenticity." I paused before plunging ahead. She needed to hear all of it. "His full name is Justin Cummings."

She yanked her hands from mine, reeling back. "Professor Cummings, then? That's who gave your agency my name?"

"Yes, but it's not what you're thinking. He admires you, Tori. He only gave your name because he thought you were the last person to accept a bribe if you were—" I paused.

"If I were what, Mitch?"

"Captured."

"You mean, that was a possibility when you asked me to leave my life here to pursue an accounting internship that doesn't even exist?"

Her voice was rising, and I caught David's concerned look from across the room. Shaking my head gently, I focused on Tori as her hands moved up to cup the top of her head.

"Is this all a game to you? My life? Sebastian's? I let you into my home—into our lives," she said as her eyes rose to meet mine. "You know my history. Jay. Sean. The lies. How could you?"

And there it was. The loathing I had dreaded seeing stamped across her face. The face that merely hours ago had lit up when she had seen me at her front door, waiting to whisk her and Sebastian off to an exciting new adventure. "Tori, sweetheart, please. I never meant to—"

"Don't. The jig is up. I'm not your sweetheart, Mitch. Your sister is safe. You no longer need to manipulate me or Sebastian to go along with your plans. The only thing I need from you now is a way to get us out of the mess you created."

Noting the resolute set of her chin, I nodded and moved to the other side of the desk, gesturing for David to join us.

"I may have met you under false pretenses, Tori, but there's nothing fake about how I feel about you or Sebastian. But I'll respect your wishes. For now."

"The amount of information I could find here on any weapon made from the 12th century until now is enough to keep me happy until retirement," David said as he took a seat.

"Yeah, me too," I grinned. "But before that can happen—for me, at least—we need to finish out this mission. And although Ana and Justin are now in the United States, the danger is, too."

"From whom? Surely not Mikaela and Christoff Blanc? We neutralized those threats before we drove out here."

Thinking again of the spoiled beauty and her white-collar crime lord father, I felt a tightening in my gut. Mikaela had threatened Tori and Sebastian's life, but it was the picture of Christoff patting Sebastian's head that nearly sent me in a tailspin. I should never have put them in this position. The guilt wasn't a new feeling, but the realization that I wouldn't make the same decision now, was.

"We merely bit off one of Hydra's heads. Christoff Blanc is a small part of a very large, very lengthy investigation. One that until recently, has been successful at frustrating the collective efforts of several counterintelligence agencies, including our own."

David whistled. "And how is your father wrapped into all of this?"

"Because he was one of the first in our agency to gather intelligence on it."

"What? Your dad was an officer, too? You never told me this either, man. I know we're international men of mystery and all that, but this is taking it a little bit to the extreme," David grumbled. "I mean, the stories I told you about my mom and dad were real."

"And what I told you and Tori about my parents was everything I knew about them until just moments ago."

"Phew. I thought my family had trust issues."

"This doesn't explain why I can't return to my home," Tori interjected. "Or who it is we are in danger from."

"Because Ana discovered information that can finally bring this entire operation to a close. And the last time someone got this close to shutting it all down, my mother was found dead on a highway, clutching a lock of what she thought was her husband's hair."

She stilled. "I'm so sorry. Why—?"

"She thought she was on her way to rescue him. My mom worked for the CIA before I was born. After she retired, she received a packet containing instructions for her to meet someone that we can only guess she assumed she'd had a run-in with in the past. It also stated if she came alone to answer a few questions, then my dad wouldn't come to any harm. A lock of his hair was used as a warning. Whoever was behind it told her that more of him would be arriving if she failed to comply."

"Did they even have him?"

"No."

"Whose lock of hair was it, then?" Tori asked, her nonchalant tone belied by the change in her posture.

"Mine."

Her forehead puckered before smoothing into a mask of stone. "And you think they'd do the same with us?"

Lifting some papers on my father's desk, I took a small envelope from out of the pile and slid it wordlessly toward Tori.

She picked it up, looking from David to me. Reaching inside, she pulled the contents out, her hands trembling. Her gasp filled the study as the envelope slid to the floor.

David swept in to grab it but she reached it first.

She lifted the flap open to replace the contents and stared wordlessly before lifting her fingers out. They shook as she closed it again.

"Yes, Tori, I do. Because, as you see, they already have."

Chapter Seven

─────── ❦ ───────

Tori

I DIDN'T REMEMBER MUCH of the walk back to my room. My mind still felt locked in the horror of what I had pulled out of the envelope.

Even though Mitch said the satiny lock of hair hadn't been identified yet, I knew it was Sebastian's. I had been running my fingers through his hair every day for the past five years. Mitch hadn't, and I could see from his face that he knew, too. When I said as much, he had nodded, his green eyes showing an empathy I wasn't ready to accept.

It was his fault Sebastian was in danger now.

Dreading the coming conversation but determined not to panic Liz any more than necessary, I wiped the moisture from my eyes as I reached our room's door.

Tapping lightly before opening it, I managed a small smile at the sight that greeted me. Liz was sitting cross-legged on my bed, surrounded by an assortment of goodies that would make a success out of any kid's sleepover.

One particular goodie stood out. "I call dibs on the blueberry muffin."

"Please, do," Liz laughed. "I told Mrs. H and Lottie it was too late for the boys to eat and there was no way you and I were going to finish these."

"Yeah, David and I tried to ward them off earlier, with much of the same success. Are the boys OK?"

"They can barely keep their eyes open. Sebastian is holding out for you, I think."

Crossing to open the cracked door adjoining our rooms, I was rewarded with a "Mom! You're back!" from the closest form tucked under the covers.

"Hi, Ms. McKinley," Drake said sleepily before turning a shoulder to us.

"Hi, boys. Just coming to tuck you in and say goodnight."

Sitting next to Sebastian, I leaned toward him, rustling his hair. I tried to shut out the alarm the action produces. Resentment for the loss of comfort this usually brought rose before I forced it back down. Smiling instead, I said softly, "Goodnight, bud. I love you."

"I love you more, Mom," he smiled.

"No way. I love you most."

I waited until his dark lashes fluttered shut before walking noiselessly out.

"You're right, Liz, they're done." Sitting on the nearest chair to remove my shoes from my aching feet, I added, "And so am I."

"I bet! I can see from your face you found something out, Tori, but it can wait another half hour, I'm sure. Why don't you take a soak in that big tub? I've got plenty here to keep me company," she laughed.

The thought of submerging myself in warm, weightless splendor was so tempting, it took a good five seconds to shake my head. "No, the bath can wait. As tired as I am, I'm afraid the experience would be lost on me. I'll wash up a bit and change into something comfortable. We have a lot to discuss."

"I don't think I like the sound of that. But go ahead. Get comfy."

"You're the best."

My clothes in hand, I plodded into the bathroom. The site of the soaking tub elicited a groan. *One day soon, I will wade in that mini-pool,* I promised myself before starting my night ritual.

***

"Wow, so you went all the way in eleventh grade, huh? I never would have pictured you as the type, Liz," I teased. I envied that her first time was with someone like David. If he was anything like the capable, good-natured man he presented himself as now, then it wasn't hard to see the appeal. He seemed like one of the good ones. And I'd be willing to bet he was still head over heels for my gentle friend.

"I just knew he was the one for me," she lamented. "But like I said, at some point, he decided I wasn't what he wanted."

"Hmm. I don't get it, though. I mean, he looks at you like you're the first-place prize of a competition he's dying to win. Did he give you any hint at all?"

"No. Just that line about it all being for the best and that I'd understand one day when I was sitting around the fire surrounded by my children."

A wistful comment David had made about a life with kids being exciting echoed through my head. It had been the day he stopped by to look for his father's watch. At least, that's what he had said he was doing. Considering what I knew now, I realized I had given him the perfect chance to do some spying on my house, if that's what he had intended. *You have watched way too many spy flicks, Tori.*

And yet, here we were. Sighing, I knew it was time. Liz needed to know.

"I guess now is as good a time as any to give you the news."

"What news?"

"We can't go home right now. In fact, it may be quite a while."

"W-hat? Why? Did something happen to our homes?" she asked, confusion dotting her features.

"No, but something could happen to one of us. Or the boys," I answered grimly. "Liz, Mitch isn't an accounting professor or department head. And David isn't a writer."

"I gathered that."

"Ana is Mitch's sister. But she, David, and Mitch are all officers of the CIA."

"So, he did it, after all," she breathed, a small smile curling her lips.

"Did what?"

"Got a job away from home, away from his family's expectations. He always clashed with his dad over that stuff. I'm glad David prevailed."

"Considering we are all in danger right now because of that job, I'm afraid I'm not as enthused. The reason we can't go home is because our houses are being watched. Mitch said that we have been under surveillance for a while."

"By whom? The CIA?

"No. Likely by more than one person who doesn't want the information that Ana has to be disclosed."

"Now I'm more confused than ever."

Sighing, I rubbed my forehead, wishing Liz had sat in on the meeting with Mitch and David. She didn't even know about Mikaela Blanc and our run-in with her and her father.

Grabbing a couple pillows from the top of the bed, I positioned them to support my upper body and settled into a comfortable spot. *This was going to take a while.*

Chapter Eight

─────────── ◈ ───────────

Mitch

I'D SAY THAT WENT well," David said, a lopsided grin belying the grim truth.

"If by that you mean we still have all of our body parts attached, then yeah, it was a huge success." Leaning toward the felt-covered table, I drew my cue back before sending it flying into the cue ball. When three balls sank into opposite pockets, I allowed a self-satisfied smile before looking up at my suddenly more focused opponent. "Sorry, I'm a bit rusty."

"Clearly," he said as I missed the next shot.

Chuckling, I looked around the room while David made short work of the table. After the excitement of the past couple of hours, I wasn't in the mood for pool anymore.

"Let's check out the rest of the space."

"I thought you'd never suggest it."

We were both quiet as we examined the room that extended down the length of the house. A man could get lost in a place like this.

I'd been in many fine homes throughout my career. Most of the women I had been assigned to seduce were the wives, girlfriends, and daughters of the world's elite. I had seen inside glittering ballrooms, cavernous dining rooms, and sumptuous bedrooms. My father's idea of a gentleman's lounge held its own amongst them.

The entire lower level was dedicated to pleasurable pursuits. From two pool tables to an L-shaped bar equipped with more top tier liquor than a five-star hotel lounge, it had the bare bones of every man's dream den. Where it blew past them was in the adjoining rooms.

Glass walls enclosed a home gym that any modern-day gladiator would be comfortable in. A rock-climbing wall took up one side of the room while the other was home to agility hurtles, a power rack, and an enormous monkey bar set with steep beams. Free weights arranged neatly in a corner were almost an afterthought in the room guaranteed to give even elite force soldiers a satisfying workout.

Across from it was a mini bowling alley that I knew would thrill Sebastian and Drake. A theater room with rows of reclining chairs positioned behind two couches was also an expected find in today's nouveau rich homes, although the addition of individual headrest screens with ear pods took it to another level. If you didn't like the main feature, you could quietly watch something else. *Brilliant.*

The final area, which took up a third of the space, was the indoor pool and grotto. It was this that had me lamenting, "I get the pool, but now that I know my father isn't the Lothario I thought he was, it doesn't seem to fit his profile."

"You're right, son, it's not really my style," my father's voice sounded from behind me.

He is eerily good at sneaking up on me, I thought, irritated.

"But I had it made to keep a promise to your mother," he continued. "If you get a chance, take a look inside. I came in search of you boys to let you know I've contacted an old colleague. He was involved in the early investigations that included Christoff Blanc's companies. I'll be meeting with him to see what he knows that might lead us to the perps threatening Ms. McKinley. Ana is coming along but then we're escorting her back to the San Francisco area for a meet-up with some of your superiors to discuss the information she has."

"Jax?"

"He's one of them. Although, I'm going to have a word with him concerning this seemingly lifelong commitment he's made to the agency," he chuckled.

"So, you do know him?" I asked, intrigued.

"Who the hell do you think I've gotten reports on you and your sister from all these years?" he scoffed before turning to David. "Take care of this hardhead, David. There might just be a 14th century Gothic Ballock dagger in your future if you do."

"Yes, sir!" David stared after his retreating back.

We were both silent. Jax was sending reports on us to my father? For several years? I didn't think things could be any stranger than what the past 48 hours had shown, but clearly, I was wrong.

"C'mon David, I need to catch Ana before she leaves."

"Now that I know you might be heir to all this, I'm at your command, sir."

Smartass. "You forget, Ana may be, too."

"Ah man, you're right," he rubbed his chin. "Hey, how serious would you say she is with that Justin fellow?"

I punched him in the shoulder hard enough to elicit a grunt. "Actually, he's one of the things I need to talk to her about. You can ask her yourself. Oh, and make sure you tell her why."

"Are you crazy?" he said, grinning wide and rubbing his arm. "She hits as hard as you do; except she's not as old, so it's harder to see them coming."

"Remind me of that the next time we're sparring."

"See, I told you you're old. Already needing me to remind of you of things."

"David," I gritted ahead of a laugh. We made it to the top of the hidden staircase that Viernan had shown us from behind a part of the study's bookshelves.

Ana's voice rang out from the other side.

"Where are those two? I didn't see them walk out of the room," her exasperated voice echoed through the wall.

Pulling the lever Viernan had told us was the way back out, the door slid open to reveal my sister crouched into a defensive stance.

"Shit, you two scared me!" she breathed, relaxing. Instantly, her expression changed and her eyes lit with interest. "A hidden passageway? That is so cool! Where does it go? A dungeon? Secret torture room?"

"Sorry to disappoint you, sis, but it's just an underground game room for adults."

Seeing her crestfallen look, I relented, "Which happens to have an impressive gym, theater, bowling, and pool room. And of course, the two things every man room has to have."

"A stripper pole and videogames?" she asked, batting her lashes.

"No, but maybe if we talk to Dad, he'll—"

Ana punched my shoulder in the same spot I had just punched David. *He's right, she does hit hard*, I thought, grinning.

"Billiards and a fully stocked bar," David chimed in.

"Well, you two have fun with that. I've got to give Jax and some suits a presentation of the money trail I was able to dig up at the Embassy. If we don't move soon, there won't be a need for any of it. Three key players have already turned up dead. I didn't spend six months holed up in a safe house for nothing."

"Copy that. I wanted to ask where Justin was now? You told me he was going to reunite with his grandfather, but if these guys have had eyes on Tori and Liz, it's possible they've had eyes on Arthur, too."

"I know. The agency is setting Arthur up somewhere safe for a little while. The main semester is over, and he'll have an assistant professor taking over his summer classes. I'm meeting Justin and Arthur at the safehouse and then following whatever orders Jax and the boys decide on. I'll keep in touch the usual way."

Reaching out to pull her close, I breathed in the spicy scent of her hair. "See that you do. And take care of yourself, kid."

"I'm only two years younger than you, old man," she laughed into my chest.

Pulling back, I saw the moisture threatening to fall from her lashes. "Then listen to your elder," I retorted. "I expect to see you at my retirement party."

"Wouldn't miss it. Especially now that the Emerald Raven has fallen. Oh, and not that you care, but I like her." And with a jaunty wave, she bounced out of the room.

Chapter Nine

―⁂―

Tori

"**M**OM, I'M TIHED OF staying in the woom!" Sebastian pouted the next morning, Drake echoing his displeasure.

Sending Liz a conspiratorial smile, I reached over to tousle his hair. "It's 'room' Sebastian and trust me when I tell you I know exactly how you feel!"

Liz laughed. "I wonder if anyone else is up? I'm looking forward to whatever Mr. Blasson has in store for us."

"I don't know but the possibilities are enough to tempt me out of here. What do you guys say?"

"Yeah!"

"Let's go!"

In the hallway, I took in the details that I was too distracted to see yesterday. The amount of light coming through, even here on the top floor, was a lot to take in at any time of the day. In the early morning hours before our eyes had adjusted, it was blinding.

We passed several large paintings, most of them Mediterranean scenes. A similar theme of mosaic tiles, arched doorways, and ornate columns was littered throughout the home's décor. The warmth of the interior was at complete odds with the cold, formidable exterior, but I liked the effect.

"Oh, you're awake!" Mrs. H. beamed up at us as we descended the stairs. "Perfect timing, too. Mr. Blasson has outdone himself this morning. Wait until I show you young gentleman what our chef has provided for your breakfast! I swear it will turn you two into strapping young men or my name isn't Mrs. Henrietta Hunt!"

"Did someone say breakfast?" Mitch inquired, entering from the direction of the great room.

Holy moly. Thoughts of food disappeared as a different hunger arose. Taking in Mitch's damp hair, I couldn't stop my eyes from sweeping slowly down his form. He was clad in a black muscle shirt that showed off everything from the corded glory of his shoulders to the knotted slopes of his biceps and forearms. Raking my eyes lower, I was rewarded with a view of muscular thighs and rounded calves.

"I hope so," David said, materializing from behind Mitch. "I haven't worked out that hard since the last time we were discussing a certain lady and—oh, good morning Tori," he greeted me. "Liz, boys. How did last night go for everyone

Liz stared at David's equally exposed body before glancing away. Her only answer was a noncommittal sound which bordered on a grunt.

"I took a bath in a huuuge tub!" Sebastian cried.

"Me too," Drake said, not to be outdone.

"Very cool. And what about your moms?" Mitch asked, his eyes crinkling.

"They took showahs! But mom wants to swim in the pool," Sebastian offered.

"So Mrs. H. beat me to telling you about downstairs, huh?"

Sebastian wrinkled his forehead in confusion.

"I made a comment to Sebastian yesterday that the bathtub is so big, it looks like a mini pool. I have every intention of soaking in it at some point today," I filled in.

"Ah, well, I'm happy to offer you the chance to soak in something even larger. My father has converted the lower level of the house to an adult playground of sorts. The pool is Olympic-sized and has some unique features. Of course, there are a few things that will make these two little scamps happy, too," he said, clapping both boys on the back. "But we can explore that later. We better sit down before Mr. Blasson gets offended and refuses to make us any more food."

"After you," David stepped aside to allow Liz and I entrance.

Resolute, I ignored Mitch when he pulled out the chair between him and Sebastian. I intended to move to Sebastian's other side but was thwarted when Liz took the seat, instead.

She refused to look me in the eye.

My watered-down smile earned a wink from Mitch. He dared a gentle caress against the back of my arm as he pushed my chair forward. The shiver that traveled down to my fingertips was not as unwelcome as it should have been. *This man is the reason you are all hiding out here instead of relaxing safely at home. Get a grip, Tori.*

Lottie entered with a large carafe. "I've made some fresh orange juice. Would anyone like some?"

A chorus of "yes's" sounded from around the table.

Finally looking at the large spread of food displayed in polished serving ware, I was amazed to find a restaurant menu's worth of variety. Belgian waffles, fluffy and lightly browned sat next to an egg, sausage, and cheese casserole large enough to feed a family of twenty.

David lifted the lid of one steaming tray to reveal an assortment of potatoes that had Sebastian squealing in delight.

"Mom! They have hash browns!"

"I see that, bud. Make sure you eat some fruit, too. Miss Liz has a bowl full of them here. There's strawberries, cantaloupe, watermelon, kiwi, apples, and grapes!"

"Ahh, mom."

"What! You don't like fruit?" David asked, his eyes wide as he reached for the bowl sitting between him and Liz. "Only the strongest warriors eat these. I just assumed you two knew that already."

"David's right. They are the first thing I eat in the morning and the last thing I eat at night. Just between you and me, I think I'd only be able to take out one or two bad guys at a time if it weren't for the power that fruit and vegetables give me."

"I want some!" the boys chanted in unison and Liz and I shared a bemused smile. To look at them loading up their plates now, you'd never guess the amount of sulking and whining we had grown used to hearing when asking them to eat just one piece.

Something solid brushed against my leg and I glanced under the table, finding Mitch's leg an inch from mine. Looking up, I caught two emeralds sparkling down at me. My breath hitched. He leaned closer until I could no longer tell where his breath ended and mine began. "We have a lot to discuss. Meet me in the study after breakfast. Make sure you're alone."

It took a second to formulate a coherent thought. "And how, exactly, am I supposed to manage that?" I asked, my eyes sweeping across the table's occupants. "You may not spare a thought for my son and friends, but I certainly do."

I regretted the words as soon as I saw his smile fade. He leaned back before saying softly, "Like I've told you before, I'll take care of this. Of you, Sebastian, and your friends, if you'll let me."

His head turned toward David before I could make a scathing reply.

He lied to you. He put you, your son, and your friends' lives at risk. Don't be fooled by his charm. The reminder was becoming a daily mantra.

So why did it feel increasingly like an empty one?

Chapter Ten

Mitch

HELL'S FIRE SHE WAS stubborn! I leaned back from the table to observe the frustrating woman I had grown to care for. It wasn't easy giving her space to grieve for the man she thought I was, but she deserved at least that.

Watching her laugh with Liz, I acknowledged my own grief. As soon as my father had explained the scope and longevity of the investigation, I realized I had been fooling myself. If the perpetrators weren't caught, and it was unlikely at this point that they all would be, then I could never offer Tori and Sebastian the safe, normal life in retirement that I had hoped for. Which meant I would never have the life I had dared to dream of. The best I could do now was offer them my protection. I just hoped it was enough.

With those morose thoughts, I pushed my chair back and stood up. All eyes turned on me and I glanced at David. "Well, I think we can all say that Mr. Blasson is one of the wonders of the world. It would be a shame to not take advantage of such talent, don't you agree, Tori? Liz?"

"Take advantage?" Tori asked.

Mrs. H and Lottie appeared as if on cue.

"Boys, how would you two like to help Mr. Blasson and Miss Lottie here make some cookies for dessert tonight?" Leaning closer, I gave them my best stage whisper, "And I've heard that Miss Lottie lets her helpers taste a couple cookies after they've cooled. But don't let Mr. Blasson know!"

Lottie laughed into her hand.

"Yes!"

"Aw Mom, can I, please?"

Mrs. H clicked her tongue, "Young Mr. Ravenschall, you're a devil, you are," she tittered before standing up straighter. "Young men, if your mommas won't mind letting me steal you away for a little while, Mr. Blasson will be happy to have your help."

Liz smiled, already nodding her head. "I'm sure they'd be delighted, if you're sure none of you mind."

"Not at all, ma'am! It's a rare treat having young ones running around this giant house. My own children are all grown with families of their own. They're so scattered about, I only get to see my grandchildren a few times a year. Mr. Blasson is still young, though," she said, looking slyly at Miss Lottie. "It'll be good practice for him, I'm thinking."

"Yes!" Drake whooped, sliding his chair out and distracting me from the fascinating pink stains spreading across Miss Lottie's face.

Turning my head to Tori, I watched the lines on her forehead deepen as she realized she would now be free to meet me in the study.

She sighed and then released a breath, "I'm OK with it if you and Lottie are, Mrs. H."

"Woohoo! Thanks, Mom!" Sebastian jumped up, turning to high-five Drake.

"Don't you fret, Ms. Tori, I'll make sure they're kept busy instead of causing mischief. Alright young men, off to work we go!" Mrs. H commanded with a smile, guiding her eager assistants toward the kitchens.

David took the sudden opportunity to address Liz. "I was hoping you still like gardening. I've been told there is an amazing garden to the back of the property."

"I-I-" Liz looked desperately at Tori. Seeing nothing but a frown on her friend's face, she continued, "Yes, I do. I'm surprised you remember that."

"Oh, you'd be surprised what I remember," he returned, winking.

I caught a slight curl of her lip through the curtain of her hair. "Ahem, yes. Well, lead the way."

As the two of them exited the dining room, I turned my attention to Tori, who was playing with an edge of her napkin and gnawing on her lip.

I let the silence build, tension increasing with each second. I was lost in the memory of how that lip felt when it had been my teeth closing around the soft flesh. How her mewling sounds had ignited a fire in me that first night I had saved her from an attack. And later, when I had plunged into her warmth, marking her as mine with each stroke.

And she was going to stay mine, as soon as I convinced her it was in her best interest.

Some of my thoughts must have shown on my face because her eyes widened while her hand fluttered to the open vee of her floral top.

I think it's time we move things to a more discreet place, I thought while willing away the hard-on hell-bent on making its presence known.

"Shall we?"

She ignored my proffered hand, sliding her chair back on the tile floor. "After you."

"Oh, no. After you." I returned her frown with a lift of my lips.

There was no way I was missing out on the view.

Chapter Eleven

Tori

NOW I KNOW WHOSE side Mrs. H and Miss Lottie are on. Help with cookies. Funny how they both showed up just as we finished eating and right when Mitch suggested we take advantage of Mr. Blasson's expertise. I'd bet everything that he and David had orchestrated the entire thing.

Realizing I was outpacing Mitch by quite a few steps, I willed myself to calm down as I reached the study doors. The handles refused to turn beneath my hand.

Keys rattling as he took them from his pocket, Mitch flashed a smile. "My father left the keys with me while he and Ana are gone for a few days."

"You two seem on good terms now. Despite everything else, I'm happy for you, Mitch."

"Thanks. I'm still getting used to it."

Swinging the doors open, he gestured for me to enter. My eyes settled on the desk that reminded me so much of the one in his office at SFSU.

"There's something I've been curious about for a while. Your office at school was so different from all the others. Was that your doing…or something that was already there?"

He looked startled by the question. "It was arranged by the agency. All I asked for was an office that had sturdy furniture with personality and none of the coldness of a traditional office. If I was getting buried in paperwork, I wanted it to be in surroundings that wouldn't make it even more hellish. It's funny, I never thought to ask," he mused. He turned his head to look at his father's desk, an arrested look on his face.

"Oh. It just didn't seem like your style. Although, I guess I don't really know what your style is…" The depressing thought threatened the fragile peace between us.

"I'd like to remedy that."

I was caught in his snare, unable to look away.

"I prefer wood to plastic, functional pieces over decorative; although ornate wood carvings are a special interest."

"And you are not a fan of doilies, white-washed furniture, lace…"

"Oh, now that's where you're wrong, Tori. I happen to have a special fondness for lace."

My face flamed as I realized too late what he was referring to. *Of course, he likes lace*, I chided myself. Who would have known it made such an effective restraint?

A man who seduced women for a living, that's who.

"I'd be more than happy to reassure you of that fact." He was standing several feet from me but the raw need I could feel just beyond his veneer of control was electrifying.

I took a step back, reaching a hand behind to anchor me. "I-I believe you."

"Good," he said with alacrity. "Then I'd love to explore more of this 'getting to know one another better' downstairs if you're up for it?"

His arrogant grin snapped me back to my senses. "Of course."

Nodding his head, he walked past me to stand in front of a bookcase at the far corner of the room. He reached up, pulling a book off the shelf and replacing it with his hand. The bookcase began to move.

As a staircase was revealed, I looked at Mitch in wonder. "Fireplace spikes and now a hidden staircase? Is there a torture chamber downstairs, too?"

His eyes crinkled, "I'm sure I could think of a few ways it could be used as one."

Rolling my eyes but grinning, I stepped toward the staircase. "This leads to the indoor playground you were talking about earlier, I take it?"

"It does."

"I'm not sure this is a good idea, to go down alone with you."

"It is."

Exasperated, I stepped through the opening, despite my misgivings. "Of course, you would say that. I'm just going because I'm curious what's down there."

"Understood."

His thinly contained laughter made me want to turn around and walk out the study doors, leaving him to his own company. But I meant what I said, curiosity had chased all other misgivings away.

Walking down the curved, cement stairs, I had the feeling I was walking in an old castle, perhaps down the steps inside a tower. The recessed lights that illuminated the way spoiled the image a bit. Cami would love it here, with her talks of Druid ancestors and magic. *Speaking of which, Tori, you need to call her. There is going to be hell to pay,* my conscience warned me.

I heard the door click shut from the top of the stairs and the skin on my arms prickled. Reaching the tile floor, I turned back to see Mitch directly behind me. "There's a way out of here, I'm assuming."

"Yes, but I'm not sure you're going to like it. Well, scratch that, I know you'll love it, but I'm not sure you'll let yourself find out," he said caustically. His face was cast in partial shadow by the dim lighting, but his mouth was on full display.

"I'll reserve judgment for now. So, time for the tour?"

He stood rigid for a moment longer before relaxing and offering me his arm. This time, I was foolish enough to take it.

Chapter Twelve

~

Mitch

"**G**O AHEAD, I'VE GOT you. Two more feet and you've made it to the end," I encouraged Tori, standing within an arms-length away from her enticing backside. I watched in torment as it swung in front of me while she made her way down the last few rungs of the monkey bars. Not for the first time, I wished she had accepted my invitation to play pool. A sudden picture of Tori bending over the table to reach a ball, her breasts dangling just above the felt table, was enough to change my mind.

The truth was, now that I'd had a taste of her, she wasn't safe from me. Anywhere.

"I did it!" she said, the smile of triumph settling perfectly on her lips as she dropped back down to the mats.

"I knew you would. I've seen you when you're determined to do something and would never be foolish enough to bet against you."

"It helped to know you were there if I fell." She refused to meet my eyes.

Her reluctance pulled at something within me. I reached her in two strides. She looked up, her eyes widening as I leaned in close enough to smell the faint hint of syrup on her breath. "And as soon as you realize I always will be, perhaps we can move past this impasse."

Her features changed in a flash. "Always is a long time. And in what form will you be there, I wonder? As Professor Mitch Logan? No, he's just a short-term player. The secretive, jet-setting Raven, perhaps? Hmm, I believe he's retiring, so that leaves us with…right, Logan Ravenschall. Now, he sounds like any woman's dream, an heir to an apparently impressive security service and supply empire with a lot of spare time to burn. The only problem is, I don't know who the hell he is," she bit out. "And you're telling me I should just trust my life, my son's life to this stranger? A man who has made a living out of lying? A man who listened to me tell my sob story of marrying not one, but two liars and told me I could t-trust h-him all the while telling me the biggest lies of all?" She broke down at this, stepping back and burying her face in her hands.

Although her explosion was expected, and necessary if we were ever to move past this, the amount of shame I felt wasn't. "Tori, you know I didn't have another choice. I was desperate to get Ana back—"

"So, you put me in danger…put my son in danger? My friends? For what? So, you can play spy games and act the hero?" Her voice dropped to a whisper. "You don't care about anyone, do you?"

"You're wrong. Those of us who do this job have to care about something. When they don't, greed and power get in the way. Tori, I swear to you, this was never an easy decision. If it wasn't for Ana, I would never have—"

"Never what? Done what you've been doing for an entire career? Lied? Coerced someone into doing what you wanted? Pretended to be someone else? I think you're fooling yourself."

I was speechless. For once, I had no idea what to say to someone to make them do what I wanted them to do. Just recognizing that thought proved her right. I'd relied on the belief that I was always working for the greater good to bypass any second thoughts about the morality of my actions. Normally, the assets I had groomed all knew what they were doing...or at least understood the danger they were in. Tori had been blindsided.

"For three years now, it has been me and Sebastian. I told myself after Sean died that I would protect him from anything or anyone who came into our lives that could possibly harm him. If that meant that I had to remain celibate, then so be it. He didn't ask for the screw-ups that his parents made." She kicked at the edge of the mat. "And then you came along, playing the knight. You saved me from one of the most terrifying attacks of my life—one I don't even know now if it was real? You chased after me when I ran like hell from the fear that somehow, I wasn't good enough for you. Then you hooked me in by cradling my son as if he was the most precious thing you'd ever had in your arms.

I watched as you charmed my friends because they were fooled by you, too. Because they hoped as much as I did that you were finally a man I could depend on. And all the while, you were just a man with a file on a woman you and your agency thought was gullible enough to use for your own purposes. I never stood a chance, did I?" she laughed bitterly. "Well, the jokes on you. I refuse to give up my freedom and safety for something I never agreed to in the first place. If you and the agency don't figure out a way to fix this, and I mean soon, I'll take my story to the press and I don't give a damn how it affects your mission. You will give me back what you have taken, Mitch."

Her defiance— even amidst her pain—was formidable. "Tori, the attack on you in the parking garage was not of our making. Yes, I had a file on you. It told me where you grew up, what your GPA was in high school, even the first car that was registered to you. None of that prepared me for your strength, for your compassion, or your bravery. The agency did not pick you, I did. If you want revenge against someone, let it be me. Going to the press and blowing wide an investigation that has been going on for decades will not change that. It would only put more innocent lives, like yours, Sebastian's, Liz's and Drake's, at risk."

Her eyes haunted, she walked over to a small cabinet stuffed with white towels rolled into perfect spirals. Lifting one up to wipe the sweat from her face, she remained silent.

Knowing the worst was past us, I decided to wait her out. If she chose to forgive me, it must be on her terms. I owed her that much.

"Why, Mitch? Why did you choose me? And don't give me the reasons you think I want to hear. Tell me, really, why you picked me to go along on this mission. What was I supposed to do for you? I deserve to know."

"You're right, you do. And I can tell you some of it, but I can't tell you all, Tori. Not until the mission has been completed or I get word from Jax that it has been aborted."

"Fine, tell me what you can."

"Ana went on assignment to collect financial data from the U.S. Embassy and Consulates in Brazil that would prove that some of the officials, and others, were knuckle-deep in a sex slave ring. The agency has been investigating it on and off for decades. Her boyfriend, Justin, wanted to go with her in case something went wrong. He's not an agent, just a marine biologist she met while on assignment at a conference he was attending. As you now know, Justin is also the grandson of your former professor, Arthur Cummings, who showed up at our agency's doorstep wanting to know, very loudly, 'where the hell we had made off with his grandson to' after he found a note Justin had left behind. Ana and Justin had both disappeared shortly after Justin managed to get a message to us that Ana's identity had been compromised. When I found out, I was ready to rip out the throat of every man there until I found out where she was. Ana's all I've got and before Justin, I was all she had, too. Jax convinced me to wait, told me I could lead a rescue mission with the backing of any resources I needed if I laid low until they gave me the greenlight."

I took a moment to scan her face, wondering what she was thinking. Her stoic expression revealed nothing, and I continued, "Six months is how long it took them to approve it. When they did, they gave me two weeks to come up with an asset—someone we could send there on a decoy assignment that would make the perpetrators curious enough to pay attention to, but not alarmed enough to put Ana or the rest of us in danger. Including you and Sebastian, Tori. When you decided to bring Liz and Drake, I decided to bring David to ensure their safety, too."

"Professor Cummings gave you my name, you said. Were there others?"

"There were ten other potentials, nine of whom I saw before you."

"And I was your choice. Why?"

"Most of them had been chosen by the agency for their paper stats. None of their personalities would have been a good fit. Too flighty, too into partying, just too young. You and the last person I saw were recommended for personality traits. Steady, bright, dependable."

"And both by Professor Cummings, I take it."

"Yes. He had a vested interest in making the process as smooth and quick for me as possible. The sooner I found our decoy—"

"The sooner you could send them into unknown danger."

"As much as you may hate me for saying this, I would choose you again, too. Although this time, I'd tell you what you were getting yourself into and hope like hell you'd want to help me save the most important person to me in this world. Which, contrary to what you might think now, is not myself," I finished with a grin, willing her to share in the joke.

I was rewarded with a twitch of her lips. The relief from that tiny, solitary movement threatened to overcome my control. *Remember, on her terms.*

"I can understand being willing to do anything to save your sister," she said finally. "And I can accept that Professor Cummings thought he was doing right by sending me to you like a sheep to slaughter. It lessens some of my affection for him, but I understand that he just wanted his grandson's safe return. Sebastian wasn't originally going to come with me, so I can't lay all of the blame for that on your shoulders, although that would have been the perfect time to unburden yourself of guilt, should you have felt any. What I can't forgive is that you played with my emotions to do it. Why coax my secrets? Build memories in the home I had created to help me forget the dreams of love I had thought I'd set aside..." she broke off, turning away from me, her shoulders shaking.

My pulse quickened as I took in the confession I knew I couldn't rejoice in, not like this. "Tori, I need you to turn around and face me."

"I'm not sure I can," she whispered.

"You are stronger than you know. Face me when I give you your answers so you can judge for yourself if they are true."

"We've already proven that I'm not good at spotting a liar."

"You think anyone has it down to a science? I've been trained to look for dozens of signs that the person I'm dealing with can't be trusted. So has Ana, David, my father, and my mother. We have all made mistakes anyway. My mother's cost her her life. Do you know why?"

She let out a deep breath, as if she had just become aware she was holding it. Slowly, she turned to face me. "No."

"Because we all want to connect with one another. People want to build a bond with someone that either reinforces how they view themselves or helps them present the version of who they want to be to others. Whether we like it or not, there are people who use that to their advantage. And they are ruthless in a way that the average person can't be. You can't keep blaming yourself for being one of the good guys, Tori."

"I don't, Mitch. I blame myself for being the girl who falls for the bad ones."

Stiffening, I took a deep breath. "Is that what you think of me? That I'm one of the bad guys?"

Forced air blowing from a vent was the only sound I heard. Her measured look showed no mercy and I was left wondering if this was how it felt to be interrogated and sentenced by someone that knows all of your secrets. To be judged and found wanting.

"No, I don't. And if you make me question that ever again—"

She never finished her sentence as I reached her in one step. Grabbing a fistful of her hair, I ground my mouth onto hers in a kiss meant to punish as much as it was to celebrate. The hell of waiting for her judgment was one I wasn't likely to forget.

Groaning, she stepped even closer, winding her arms around my neck to give as good as she received. Her sweet surrender had my body straining toward her, eager to show her how much she'd been missed. Yet, knowing this was just the first step in healing the rift between us, I pulled back after planting a final kiss on her mouth.

It was true that I chose her but until now, she hadn't known enough about me to choose me, too. There was still a lot for her to learn but for the moment, I would not second guess this gift.

Chapter Thirteen

———— ❦ ————

Tori

WATCHING THE FEAR IN Mitch's eyes as he awaited my answer had snapped me out of some of the anger and resentment darkening my thoughts. He was right. Though it was unlikely I'd know every time a man decided to lie to me, I could at least tell when one was interested enough to stick around through the tough times. It was always the ill-intentioned that turned tail when the waters grew rough.

He was facing my anger head-on, not gaslighting or downplaying it, but accepting it and admitting to his part in it. What more could I ask for? It had been several minutes since I admitted to myself that if it had been Cami, Eric, or Sebastian in a similar situation, I may not have had the courage to do what he had done for Ana. Desperate situations could lead to even more desperate actions.

I had answered honestly then that I didn't see him as a bad guy. Wanting to protect his sister tipped the scales much more toward the opposite direction.

His reaction to the declaration had been everything I could hope for. I had found myself caught up in a hailstorm of sensations as he had pulled me to him, his lips crushing mine. All coherent thoughts ceased as I was swept into the haven of his arms. My body pressed closer to the source of heat and a low groan had escaped from deep in my throat. I hadn't known I could miss something that I hadn't had long to get used to.

He had pulled away gently, kissing my lips as if to reassure me this was only goodbye for the moment.

Returning to the present, my eyes opened and I was relieved to see only humor sparkling from the depths of his.

"I thought it better to show you I understand, without you having to threaten the life of government property. Don't worry, it won't be long before you can rail at me all you want. As soon as I take care of your safety, I'm retiring from the CIA."

"Where will you go?" I asked as we made our way to the next room he said he wanted to show me.

"That path isn't exactly clear," he returned, looking forward.

I considered his profile a moment before choosing my words. "Look, Mitch. I can't say that everything is OK between us just because your lies stem from a more well-meaning place than the previous liars in my life. You still put us all in danger and now it feels like we're prisoners while you and the agency fix everything.

He turned back toward me, running his hands down my arms. "You have every right to your anger, Tori. I can only assure you that I won't rest until I've put your life back to rights. In the meantime, I'm asking that you don't close the door on us—on the way we make each other feel."

I wanted to tell him that I didn't think I could ignore my feelings for him no matter what he did, but I realized it was my traitorous body that was responsible for the thoughts. Even the innocent brush of his hands along my skin was electrifying. I settled for a nod.

His answering smile lit his features. "Good. Now, let me show you that large soaker tub I promised."

The smell of chorine filled the air and I could hear the telltale splashing of water, revealing the identity of the pool before we reached it. Even still, the sight of the recreated tropical setting was a delight. A faux cave sat in the middle of a rock hardscape, a waterfall spilling over the front like a privacy curtain for anyone inside.

"Wow."

"Yeah, it's pretty ostentatious. My father assures me he had it built to honor my mother. He said there is something inside I'd like to see. So, how about it?"

"What, go in there? I don't have my bathing suit on—"

"Neither do I. I'm sure we can get Viernan and Mrs. H to help with that."

I had no intention of exploring a romantic cave clad only in a bathing suit with a half-naked man I'd already been intimate with. Especially not one that I very much wanted to be intimate with again…but on my terms. Thinking fast, I realized that once Sebastian caught sight of us, he would undoubtedly demand to be included, effectively throwing cold water on any seduction plans Mitch was entertaining.

"OK, I'll go ask Mrs. H while you find Viernan, then."

"Oh, no need." Mitch reached behind my head with one arm, his chest brushing across mine. I inhaled his masculine scent, remembering the first time I had caught the intoxicating blend that was as unique as the man it adorned.

A familiar voice sounded from the intercom. "Viernan here."

"Hi, Viernan. Tori and I are downstairs at the pool. We've decided to have a swim but I'm afraid neither of us have our suits with us. Is there any way you can grab mine from the second drawer of the dresser in my room and direct Mrs. H to the—" He stopped to look at me.

"Top drawer of mine," I sighed, knowing when I'd been beaten.

"Top drawer of Tori's dresser for hers?"

"Of course, sir. Would you like refreshments brought down, as well?"

I shook my head at Mitch's inquiring look.

"No, thank you Viernan. We'll make do with what's down here," he said with a wink to me. "Oh, and one more thing."

"Yes, sir?"

"Check on those two young scamps and if they're content in the kitchens, no need to tell them our plans. Ms. McKinley deserves a little time for herself."

"Indeed, sir. I'll let Mrs. H know, as well."

"Excellent! Thank you, Viernan."

"You're welcome, sir."

"Now, where were we?" he asked, his eyes wide in mock innocence.

I smiled weakly. *I don't know but I think I'm in trouble.*

***

Looking at myself in the bathroom reflection, I noted without vanity that the black designer one piece flattered my curvy shape. The suit was a hand-me-down from Cami and featured a V-neck with slight ruffling to give the otherwise sleek design a boost of femininity. I had worn it during an impromptu swim at her house when Sebastian was out of school. As soon as I had walked out of her guesthouse, she had given a whistle.

"Don't even think about giving that suit back to me because it has claimed its rightful owner! Tori, you look incredible in that suit!"

Her praise had been a balm to my ego. After two failed marriages, especially one in which my husband announced he was more interested in his own sex, I had started to lose confidence in my appeal.

Taking a deep breath, I reached into the pocket of the shorts I had hung on the vanity and dialed Cami's number. I needed to hear her voice. And she needed to hear from me that everything was ok.

She picked up on the second ring. "Tori! What the hell is going on? Are you ok? Is Sebastian ok? Wait until I get my hands on that professor of yours!" she cried.

"Hi Cam. I'm ok. Sebastian is fine. Liz and Drake are with us, as you are aware," I said, with just a hint of pique.

"Don't you give me attitude, Pita! Eric and I have been going nuts wondering what happened to you! I had to threaten Liz with the cops if she didn't spill on why I hadn't received the 'we're boarding now' text you were supposed to send me. Then I got this horrible feeling that you all were in danger and I was this close to making Eric drive out to

LAX to look for you. Why aren't you on a plane to a romantic destination for the internship of your life?"

"I can't tell you everything right now," I half-whispered. "But Mitch isn't exactly a professor and there is no internship."

"What? Then who is he? Tori, is he dangerous? Just say the word and Eric and I will have the cops there so fast—"

"No cops, Cami, please. We're OK, I promise. We just—we just can't go home for a while. And whatever you do, stay away from my house. There might be someone looking for us, Cami. I know it's a lot to ask, but you have to trust me when I say it isn't safe for me to say more. As soon as I can, I will, though. You'll be the first person, just as you've always been."

"You're scaring me, honey," she said in a tone I'd never heard from her.

My ears were stinging from unshed tears. "I know. I'm scaring myself," I whispered. "I miss you."

"I miss you, too. Just tell me we weren't wrong about your guy."

"He was sort of forced to lie about who he is because of his job. His real job. We weren't exactly wrong about him, but he comes with more baggage than we thought."

"Don't they all?" she asked wryly.

Chapter Fourteen

———— ～ ————

Mitch

SLIPPING INTO THE RED swim shorts Viernan had brought down, I grabbed the towels he was thoughtful enough to include and entered the pool room. Pulling a couple of reclining lounge chairs closer toward the grotto area, I threw our towels onto them.

I looked down at the control pad Viernan assured me would operate everything we needed and started testing the functions. Music blared from around the room and I scrambled to turn down the volume. Decibel level under control, I switched through the stations until a familiar song came on.

Smiling, I turned to the lights, dimming the ones inside the pool to a warm amber while keeping the grotto well lit. For now. The overhead lights were also on a dimmer I was relieved to find, and I turned those down to a soft glow.

The last thing I want is to spook her on the first opportunity I have alone with her. With that thought, I threw the remote onto the stack of towels and turned to ascertain the depths of the pool. The front portion had three wide steps in a half-circle that made for an easy entrance.

The water temperature was perfect, warmer than the air-conditioned basement, but cooler than my body temperature. The effect was as enticing as it was refreshing, and I walked down the sloped floor until the water level reached my chest. Ducking underwater, I was pleased to discover the deeper area made up the rest of the pool to the cave wall. Rising to the top, I tread water as I scanned the room for Tori. Still no sign of her.

Swimming toward the steps, I paused to plant my feet as I reached shallow water. Slicking back the hair clinging to my temples, I looked up to find Tori walking through the room's doorway. I was hard in an instant.

The curves I had admired since the first day she had walked into my office were on full display. The black bathing suit that clung to them was a lucky bastard.

My eyes weren't sure what to feast on first, but they started with the mahogany hair swinging freely to her waist. The curled ends caressed the top of her hips as they swayed back and forth in tune with her steps. Her legs looked forged from a cast that only my imagination could create: slender ankles, rounded calves, and thighs built with the strength to crush a man's heart. And all that exposed skin drew my attention better than the blood-red cape of a matador.

Eyes settling on her face, I muttered under my breath, *Cool it. She looks terrified you're about to pounce on her.*

Smiling, I stated simply, "That suit could stop traffic."

She smiled back, relaxing slightly. "Thanks. It was Cami's. A little more revealing than my usual taste, but..." she trailed off, looking away.

"But you figured it would be perfect for Brazil. It's OK, Tori. I know you're disappointed and you don't have to shield that from me." Walking out of the pool to stand within arm's reach of her, I ignored the prickling of my skin in the cool air and took her hand. "Once this mess is dealt with, I will take you anywhere you want to go. Just name the place. But for now, let me offer you this as one of the few peace offerings I have available to give."

She studied me for a moment before nodding. "I'm going to put my stuff down. How's the water?"

"Heated but still cools you down." I followed her to the chairs I had pulled aside.

"That sounds heavenly."

"It is. Hey, I'm just realizing I've never asked, but what kind of music do you like?" I queried, grabbing the remote.

"Good music," she replied cheekily. "Eva Cassidy, Stevie Wonder, Jeff Buckley, Al Greene, the list goes on and on."

Searching through the stations to find one I had heard while flipping through earlier, I settled on it. The sounds of James Brown's "Try Me" filled the large room. "Good music, it is."

Her effervescent smile was my reward. "How deep does it go?"

My mouth dried. "I'm sorry, what was that?"

"The pool, how deep is it?"

"Ah, I couldn't touch bottom about a third of the way in. The deep end stretches along the entire length of the pool, so if you can't swim, let me know and I'll stay in the shallow end with you."

"Thanks, but I was on the swim team all through high school. Let me know if you can't keep up and I'll slow down for you."

With a saucy wink, she dove into the middle of the pool. The Temptations crooned from the speakers, and I grinned. "My girl, indeed."

Tossing the control pad onto the chair, I turned and dove in after her. The jolt of the water felt less welcoming this time, but my body quickly acclimated.

Treading water, I watched in admiration as Tori glided smoothly by, her hair mirroring the fluidity of her body. She was obviously at home here and the simple pleasure of witnessing her joy settled over me. I knew that feeling. It was what drew me to her from the first time we met. The feeling that I had found home.

She disappeared under the water in one smooth motion and I made my way to the tiles' edge, flipping onto my back. The weightless sensation as I reached up to grasp the cool stone caused a deep sigh of appreciation. Even this small illusion of freedom was a rarity.

A tugging on my shorts announced Tori's arrival a second before she surfaced.

Smoothing back her hair, water dripping off her eyelashes, she looked like a figure from every one of my teenage dreams.

"I had no idea how much I missed this," she said, her eyes sparkling.

"You look like a water siren, sent to entice me toward dangerous shores."

"Are you accusing me of being dangerous?"

"No, I'm accusing you of being a temptress." At her self-satisfied grin, I continued, "But I feel it's only fair to warn you that your ignoble campaign may backfire, my Lady Temptress."

"Ignoble!" she sputtered. "My intentions are completely noble, I assure you."

"Liar."

"Hmph. You were the one to suggest this little pool outing, if I remember correctly. Something about wanting to explore the grotto…"

"And yet, here we both are. *I* seem to remember a certain water nymph leading the dive into these very waters."

Laughing, she conceded, "Fair enough. And I'm not sorry I did, just so you know."

"Neither am I."

Searching her face, I noted how her gaze kept dropping to my mouth. I let go of the wall and wrapped one arm around her unresisting form. The scent of chlorine mixed with the honeysuckle shampoo of her hair as I leaned in. Wanting to savor this reunion, I captured her top lip and ran my tongue along the satin flesh. Moving to her bottom lip, I sucked it in gently while reaching down to cup her bottom. Her moan sent a message to my cock that my brain was too clouded to override.

She pulled back, her breaths rapid and shallow. "Now who's tempting whom?"

"Guilty. And just so you know, I'm not sorry I did," I echoed her earlier words.

"I'd be disappointed if you were."

"Careful, siren."

Her expression grew serious before brightening again. "Usually, I am. But since today has been offered as a gesture of peace, I have every intention of enjoying it."

"An excellent plan. Now, would you like to take a mini-adventure with me and explore the fascinating—albeit man-made—caves of Castle Ravenschall?"

"The caves of Castle Ravenschall? How could I resist such an illustrious sounding landmark?"

"I thought you'd see things my way."

We both pushed out of the water and I handed her a towel after reaching the chairs first.

"I'm curious what's inside the cave. Your dad says it has to do with your mom?"

"Yes. I'm curious, too. Although, I wouldn't want you to get your hopes up. It could be a simple memoriam plaque in her honor."

"That would be sweet enough for me," she sighed.

Making our way to the cave, we searched for the entrance. An inspection of both sides of the grotto failed to present an opening. We were both surprised to find that the length of the cave reached the back wall. I realized then that there was only one other possibility. Clearly, the waterfall wasn't just for decorative purposes.

"Unless your father intended to make this a rock-climbing adventure, the only other way we can get in is through the waterfall."

"I think you're right. Since there's already a rock-climbing wall in the gym, it seems a bit redundant to put one in here, don't you think?"

"Especially without any finger or footholds," she observed wryly. "I have to say, this is a bit more intriguing than it looked like at first glance."

"I agree. Shall we?" I offered her my hand as we stepped in front of the torrent of water.

She refused, smiling. "I've got it."

"I never doubted it. Get ready to hold your breath."

I passed through, my foot reaching textured stone as my ears adjusted from the roaring water that had muffled them. Opening my eyes, I saw Tori was beside me, flipping her hair to the side to squeeze the water from it.

"That was exhilarating!" she said loudly over the sounds of the waterfall. Her voice echoed, causing us both to erupt in laughter at the sound.

"I wonder if the echo feature came extra?" I mused, grinning as I turned to walk down the tunnel.

"All we need now are some ancient artifacts and cave drawings for the optimal adventure," her voice rang from behind me.

Spotting something on the cave walls, I stopped suddenly. Tori collided with my back and I turned, instinctively reaching out to steady her. Not taking my eyes off the walls, I stated, "Never let it be said my father fails to deliver."

Chapter Fifteen

Tori

"**W**HAT IS IT?" I asked, intrigued.

"Cave drawings," Mitch replied, his tone subdued.

Peering at the wall, I was fascinated by the stick figures and symbols etched into the faux stone. "Wow, these are so cool! They almost look like—"

"—children's drawings?" he choked out. "That's because they are. Mine and Ana's, to be exact."

Sensing the massive effort Mitch was exerting to control his emotions, I rested my hand lightly on his back. The look he shot me was raw, his eyes glistening with unshed tears. He didn't strike me as the kind of man who allowed himself this kind of release often.

"It's OK. You can let it out. I doubt you've allowed yourself to grieve for her properly, especially in light of the new information."

Knowing he was unlikely to make the first move, I turned him toward me, both arms wrapping around his wide shoulders. He stiffened before reaching down to pull me in a crushing embrace. I

97

could feel his shoulders shaking but no sound emitted from the spilling of his grief. It saddened me as I realized this may be the first time he'd been able to unburden even a portion of the fear, sadness, and anger that came with the loss of a loved one.

"Let it out. It's just you and me here," I soothed, reaching up to run my fingers through his soft hair.

We stood like this for several moments, my damp shoulder telling me he had gotten quite a bit of emoting done. A tenderness erupted from within me and I admitted the futility of trying to stay emotionally distanced from this man. He was the mixture of hard and soft, gallant knight of yesterday and tough-minded man of today, that I had been searching for.

The air in the cave grew thick and I fought off the need for distance.

"Thank you, Tori. I hadn't realized how assiduously I've been avoiding doing that," he said, backing away from me.

I breathed a sigh of relief as the distance calmed my restlessness.

"You're welcome. I know the damage it can do to your insides when you don't let the pain out."

He turned to look at the etchings again, running his hand over the uneven rays of a sun. "My mom had the originals of these displayed around the house. This was on our refrigerator until the beginning of my 8th grade year when I begged her to take it down." A smile tugged at his lips. "I was afraid one of my friends would come over and see it."

"Oh yes, that would have been a grave mistake, indeed," I teased. "At least that was one of the indignities of childhood that I escaped."

His head whipped around. "I'm so sorry. Here I am complaining of experiences your time in foster care didn't afford you."

"No, it's fine. I don't begrudge you these moments just because I didn't have them. In fact, my bedroom at home has quite a few framed pieces from Sebastian's childhood."

"Living vicariously through the parenting you provide your son?"

"Something like that. Now that we're further away from the waterfall, why do I hear the sound of more water churning?" I asked, taking a step toward the noises.

"Excellent question. I think another discovery is afoot. Lead the way."

Ignoring the prickling of his eyes from behind me, I focused on a shimmering light on the wall before a large opening appeared. In the middle of the room, a bubbling hot tub beckoned.

"You didn't request a hot spring, but I can't say I'm upset with the discovery."

Excited despite the warning bells going off inside my head, I smiled at Mitch. "I wonder if it has restorative properties?"

"Perhaps it's a fountain of youth and we will both revert back to our younger selves," he joined in.

"I hope not. I rather like who I am right now."

"So do I."

The warmth of his gaze was on par with the heat emanating from the frothy water as I stuck one tentative foot in. "Oh my. That feels incredible," I groaned, braving the other foot.

I sunk in further, the heat almost too much while my body temperature did its best to regulate itself. My head fell back and a deep sigh of appreciation escaped. The silence stretched and I wondered why

Mitch hadn't joined me. Opening one eye to peer up at him, I found his attention on me, a pained look on his face.

"What's wrong?"

"I don't think me getting in there is a good idea."

"Why not? The heat feels amazing once you get used to it."

"I'm sure it does."

"Then come in!"

"I'd like to. That's the problem."

Confused, I could only stare into his handsome face, searching for his meaning.

"If you're looking for answers, you'll have to drop your eyes lower."

I did and immediately saw what he was referring to. The front of his trunks was jutting out, barely caging in his arousal. My nerve endings came alive from breasts to heated core. Catching the breath that had stalled, I braved a look back at his face.

"If you had gotten in the water, I would never have known."

"If I get in that water, it will be all that you know," he promised.

It took a second more to realize he was giving me exactly what I wanted: a chance to do things over, on my terms. I could admit to myself that I had wanted this to happen since I agreed to go swimming. It has been torturous to be so close to him without being given another taste of his skin or to feel the weight of him bearing down on me. A rush of excitement brought a wave of heady power.

"I'm not sure I know what you mean by that." Shifting on the bench seat, I raised my body up so that the deep vee of my suit was exposed. The water caressed the underside of my breasts as the cold air hit my nipples from beneath the wet fabric. I felt them tighten in response.

"I can think of nothing I'd rather do than to show you what I mean."

Catching his intense gaze once more, I gave him my answer. "Then come show me."

He was in the water before I could shift aside to make room. It didn't matter, since he reached down to lift me from the comfortable heat, swinging my legs to straddle his hips. In an impressive feat, he sat us both down carefully in the swirling water.

The dual sensations of heat on my legs and cold air on my upper body caused a prickling of my skin. My nipples were so tight they threatened to cut through the thin fabric covering them. I wasn't cold for long as he wrapped his arms around me and pulled me in for a fiery kiss.

"I've been waiting for this, Tori," he said when he came up for air, his breath as ragged as mine. "But I wanted it to be your decision. Wanted you to choose me when you knew who I really was, not who I was pretending to be."

Trying to focus on his words when he was pulling down both sides of my bathing suit was no easy task. "I-I know. And I choose you, Logan. Here. Now." Saying his real name, the name that sounded as foreign to me as a stranger's, seemed important in this moment.

He stopped his task to grasp my face gently in both hands, bringing it close to his. "You don't know how long I've wanted to hear my name cross your lips. When we are in private, I want you to use it, Tori."

"Yes, Logan."

He leaned in for a thorough kiss that left me in no doubt of his approval.

Restlessly, I stirred in his lap, my body searching for what it craved.

"Careful, Tori," he breathed against my lips. "You're going to make this go a lot faster than you may wish for."

Smiling, I grabbed a handful of his hair between my fingers and tilted my mouth until it was poised above the full lips I knew I'd never tire of tasting. I kissed him over and over, letting my lips cling to his as each one ended. My hips began a restless dance, circling around his erection until he moaned into my mouth.

A squeal escaped as I jumped in his arms, trying to dislodge the fingers now probing between my legs.

"Shh, sweetheart. I need to feel you," he soothed, tucking his fingers underneath my suit to pull it aside. Finding the spot he was searching for, he began to circle it while two fingers slipped inside. The friction between our wet skin gave way to the slickness his questing fingers found.

His mouth trailed down my neck to stop at the sensitive spot along my collarbone. He left a firestorm of sensation along the edge of the suit's plunging neckline before letting out a grunt of impatience.

The fingers that had been wreaking havoc on my lower body withdrew and it was my turn to give voice to frustration. Fortunately, it wasn't for long as I realized his intent.

Bold hands moved to my shoulders to finish the job they had started earlier. Sliding my suit off each shoulder, he rained impassioned kisses on each new inch of skin he exposed. By the time he reached my nipples, I was bucking against him, pulling his head to the hardened tips. He took first one and then the other in his hot mouth, his tongue swirling to cup the undersides of each as his mouth pulled incessantly.

"L-logan," I groaned, lost in desire. "Please."

In answer, he took both breasts in hand, holding them together until one was within inches of the other. He looked up at me with carnal promise as he started sliding his lips between each tip, wrapping his warm mouth around one for just a second before grasping the next. How long he kept at it was beyond my scope of consciousness.

When he stopped, my moan of disappointment made him smile. Reaching between us while lifting his hips, he pushed his shorts down until the waistband rested across his thighs. The satiny length of him started rubbing against my skin and I realized my suit had shifted back to cover the tender flesh. A sigh escaped.

"What's the matter, siren? Having a little trouble getting what you want?"

I shot him a glare. "Oh, it's just something *I* want?" Planting both hands on his chest, I rubbed against his straining flesh, allowing the tip of him to push against the cloth blocking its entrance. I leaned down to tease his ears and neck with my mouth, nipping at him gently. Shifting upward, I dangled both breasts in front of his lips, moaning when he latched onto them greedily. Arching my back, I reached behind me to take his erection firmly in hand, testing its strength. The sheer size of it was enough to turn my arousal up to a blazing fire. So much for making him beg for it.

"Now."

"As you command," he said smoothly.

I saw no hint of triumph on his handsome face, only an echo of my own desire.

Grasping my hips, he lifted me up while stretching his legs to rest across the bench seats facing us, his knees slightly bent. He leaned forward, forcing me to fall against his legs. Grinning at my expression of alarm, he held my gaze as he reached a hand toward the junction of my thighs. Running a tantalizing finger along the edge of my suit, he pulled it aside once more. His thumb circled in an electrifying pattern and I let my head fall back.

My eyes closed and I let his fingers and the thoughts of what was to come send me close to the edge.

Chapter Sixteen

―~―

Mitch

SHE WAS CLOSE, I observed, watching her body tremble against my hand. My cock was so full, I knew it wouldn't take long to find my release. It was time.

Moving to the edge of the bench seat and leaning over to arrange Tori's delightfully exposed body, I positioned her plump folds against my engorged tip.

To my surprise, she took control, planting her feet on the bottom of the hot tub and pushing me back against the seat. The determined look on her face was one I knew would be etched in my memories for eternity. Tamping down on the need to drive deep inside her, I took a measured breath, thinking of anything but the fact that this sexy woman was now settling herself upon my erection.

Her feet moved to either side of my hips while her hands grasped my shoulders. I watched in torturous wonder as she dropped her hips slowly, her body swallowing nearly every inch of my delighted cock. A groan escaped us both and we shared a smile. Content to let her set the pace, I dipped my head while lifting a plump breast to meet my mouth. Suckling on it hard, I was rewarded with an increase in tempo.

Sighing inwardly, I resigned myself to the knowledge that this would not be one of my most stellar performances.

The water's heat seemed insignificant to the flames stirring inside as my release loomed near. Determined to give Tori satisfaction first, I turned my attention to her other breast and reached a hand between us, rhythmically drawing out her response. I felt her insides clench around me a moment before she cried out. Taking command of her hips, I drove into her with deep, fast thrusts before exploding inside her.

She collapsed against my chest.

A wave of tenderness hit as my heartbeat returned to its normal resting rate. Combing through her hair, I dropped a kiss along her hairline. My lips twitched at her moan of approval humming against my chest.

"I can't move," she said. "I hope I'm not too heavy."

"You're a feather," I assured her, ignoring the pain in my tailbone. I wasn't about to let her leave without providing a better showing of the pleasure I planned to give her. Often. With that thought, I shifted forward, relieving some pain while taking advantage of the position to push even deeper inside her.

Her head whipped up and she sent a heavy-lidded look at me before reaching down to kiss me. "You're still hard?" she breathed.

"Mmhm."

"Impressive."

Clinging to her lips, I warned, "You haven't seen anything yet."

We're both panting as I cupped her bottom and stood, her legs wrapping tightly around my hips.

"As delightful as it is to have your delectable body melded against mine, I have something in mind that I've been fantasizing about for a while."

"Is that right?"

"Yes. How do you feel about making a man's wishes come true?"

"Depends on the man and the wish. If that man is you, I feel fairly good about it."

"Good. Then turn around."

She studied my face and I realized I was holding my breath. What I was asking for wasn't as lighthearted as my tone implied. One thing years of experience had taught me was that a woman wasn't going to submit to a man, even in casual sex, unless some trust had been established. Trust was the building block of a relationship, and I had demolished ours.

Slowly, she loosened her grip around my hips, dropping her legs to stand between mine. I waited in silence for her next move.

"I think I should go check on the boys. They are probably giving Mrs. H a coronary by now. And if she's been brave enough to give them any of the cookies…" she trailed off with a tight laugh.

Right. Still some foundation work to be done.

"I understand. Shall we bring the boys down here? I'm sure they'd enjoy playing pool or perhaps watching a movie? I've been told there isn't a movie title they can't access here. That's likely an exaggeration, but regardless, I'm confident we can find something they'd be interested in."

"Yes, thank you. That would be wonderful, Mitch."

Permits been revoked, constructions at a halt. Sighing as she dressed in a rush, my lips twitched at a thought. *At least I come equipped with my own hardhat.*

***

"I think that kid has a future in 9-ball tournaments," David said, joining me at the bar, away from the sounds of balls clacking and children's excitement.

I watched as Liz high-fived Drake and Tori gives Sebastian a good-natured hair tousle.

"Drake seems to have a solid grasp of the game. With a little coaching, you two could grow to be a formidable duo."

"Yeah, he reminds me of me at his age. My mom said I used to bug her and Dad to go over my Uncle Eric's house because he had a pool table. She said it irked my dad because we couldn't afford one but that he felt vindicated when I got a little older and wiped the table with my uncle."

"So that's where you honed your skills."

"It's where it all started, at least. My high school had a different take on what gym class looked like. We had a pool table, foosball, and even a little TV in one corner. Of course, we had access to the gymnasium for the more traditional things like basketball, but I was a fixture at the pool table. And so was Liz," he finished softly.

"How are things going on that front?"

"Slowly. I tried to hold her hand and she pulled it away; politely, of course."

Grimacing in sympathy, I poured him a drink. "Here, drink this. It'll make it smart a little less."

"Doubtful, but I'll take it anyway," he grinned, swigging the whiskey back in one long gulp. "But you know what would help? How about some tips from the man who's made a career out of seducing women?"

"A career out of what?"

Shit. What are the odds?

I turned to find a bristling version of the woman who had been sending me sweet smiles and covert glances for the past hour. The hope that had built since our hot tub tryst crumbled in the face of her outrage.

"It's just boy's locker room talk," David waved off, throwing tinder at a flame. Of course, he didn't know what happened between Tori and I earlier, but his comment now made it seem like he did, in all its lustful glory.

"What my oh-so-eloquent friend is trying to say is that he was just busting my chops to deflect from his failure with engaging your friend's affections."

David hung his head before giving her a winning smile. "Busted. As Liz's close friend, I guess I should be asking you for tips, huh, Tori? So, any words of advice for a cloddish fellow with a heart bigger than his brain?"

Tori perused my face before turning to David. "Yes. Be honest." She flicked a dismissive glance down the length of me. "And make sure she never has to question that honesty. Your rack, David."

As she sauntered away, her shoulders stiff and backside swaying, I let out a breath.

"OK, so maybe I shouldn't be asking you for advice," David smirked before patting me on the shoulder. Pouring some whiskey into my glass, he continued, "Here, it'll make it smart a little less."

Prick.

Chapter Seventeen

―――――― ～ ――――――

Tori

SMILING DISTRACTEDLY AT SEBASTIAN'S excitement as I reached the pool table, I pondered the conversation I had just interrupted. What had David meant by wanting tips "from the man who had made a career out of seducing women"? Was that what Mitch did for the CIA? Then...

Sighing, my eyes closed as if trying to seal off the truth from the curious brain residing nearby. The implication was more than I cared to acknowledge. Pasting a smile as the men rejoined us, I made a mental note to ask Mitch exactly what his role was for the agency. Even if he couldn't tell me specifics, he should at least be able to set my mind at ease on this. And this time, without trying to deflect the answer with a fellow—and no doubt loyal—agent.

"Anyone up for a rematch?" Mitch asked.

"Yes, me! Me!" Sebastian cried, grabbing onto Mitch's t-shirt. The casual grey V-neck that clung to his muscular arms was invitation enough. I clamped my lips tightly together to keep from claiming my own rematch. It wasn't a game of pool I had in mind.

Professional seducer, Tori. And liar. And goodness knows what else. Get a grip.

Needing to get away from his magnetic pull, I turned to Liz. "Looks like the boys won't need us for a bit. What would you like—"

I stopped at the unmistakable sound of footsteps coming down the hidden staircase. Viernan appeared with his dirty blonde hair askew and an alarmed look he did his best to hide. "Mr. Ravenschall, there is a matter of grave concern I need to discuss with you." His eyes darted to the children. "In private, sir."

Mitch's frown at the odd interruption smoothed and a smile appeared. "That sounds like a burnt dinner, perhaps, which would be a grave concern, indeed," he joked, smiling at Sebastian and Drake. Shooting a harder look at David, he said, "David, I'm sure you won't mind if Sebastian takes my shot until I come back, right?"

"I should mind since he's a better player, but I guess Drake and I will do our best to fend him off until your return."

Sebastian grinned while Drake punched the air, exclaiming, "We've got this!"

Liz and I shared a worried look as Mitch disappeared up the stairs with Viernan.

"Shall we browse through the movies in the theater room for tonight's showing?" I asked her.

"Yes, if David is OK with the boys?"

David chalked the end of his pool stick before handing it to Sebastian. "Don't worry about us. We'll be busy for at least a couple of minutes," he teased, nudging Sebastian.

"You'll see!" Sebastian warned gleefully, swinging the child-size cue in front of him.

A chuckle escaped as I linked arms with Liz. "Looks like they're in good hands. Now, were you thinking action-adventure or comedy?"

"I think we've seen enough action and adventure lately," she said softly.

"Good point. Comedy it is."

As we rounded the corner of the theater room, David's encouraging words to Sebastian echoed faintly.

"So, I know we're both concerned by whatever Viernan was in such a bother about, but I think we should reserve true panic until we learn more. Deal?"

"Deal," Liz smiled. "Does that mean I can ask why you've been blushing around your would-be professor all afternoon?

"Caught that, huh?"

"Even if I hadn't, Mitch's inability to look away every time you leaned in to take a shot…"

"Uh, right. Well, we spent some time in the pool. Did I tell you I wanted to be an Olympic swimmer? I competed all through high school but realized I was missing a very important component of being a world champion."

"What was that?"

"A competitive nature." I smiled, moving to flip through a 3-ring catalog of movies sitting on a bookshelf. "I realized swimming would always be a hobby that I really enjoyed, even though I haven't had much opportunity to do even that the past several years."

"It must have felt nice to get back into the water."

"Yes, it did. I plan on spending more time enjoying it while we are holed up here. Hopefully, without the very distracting form of the man whom we shall not name."

Liz grinned before pointing out a movie in an identical binder. "I heard Drake and Sebastian talking about this one recently."

"Perfect, then we've accomplished our mission. Now, are you going to tell me what you and David were up to in the gardens, or will I have to drag it out of him instead?"

Liz's cheeks turned a pale mauve. "We started talking about the flowers and plants."

"Ah yes, and then perhaps you moved onto the birds and the bees?" I couldn't resist teasing her.

As she dipped her head, flipping through the pages of the binder again, I reached out to clasp her arm. "I'm just teasing, Liz. Just because that's where Mitch and I ended up doesn't mean I should assume you and David did, as well."

She looked up quickly, "So you two—"

"We did. And then a few moments ago, I walked in on a conversation that made me feel like a fool for doing so. But enough about me. What happened after your nature-inspired conversation?"

"David told me about the death of his mom. Oh, Tori, it was terrible, some of the things he was saying. His father practically cut him out of the family when he joined the CIA right after his mom died. He said Raven—sorry, Mitch—saved him from wallowing in depression and helped make him into the best version of himself he could be."

"High praise, indeed. I'm sorry to hear about David's dad. Have they been able to mend things?"

"Yes, I believe so. He says his father wanted him to marry a Korean woman that was a friend of the family."

"I take it David didn't feel the same? He seems like a sweetheart, but I'd never take him for a pushover."

"No," she sighed. "He didn't, and he's not. A pushover, that is."

I watched in amusement as she fiddled with the movie catalog again. "I'm happy you two have reunited. Who knows what the future holds?"

"Tori."

I swung around to face Mitch in the doorway.

"You startled me! Is everything alright?"

"I need to gather everyone together in the study. Mrs. H and Lottie are waiting upstairs to take Sebastian and Drake to see some of the exotic fish my father has in the aquarium room."

"There's an aquarium room?" I asked, distracted.

Mitch nodded, his solemn face sending warning bells down my spine. "I'll have Viernan set some refreshments in the study. However, I would suggest you pour yourselves a drink from the bar to bring up. Make it a strong one." And with that, he walked out.

"That doesn't sound good," Liz breathed, her eyes as wide as mine felt.

"No, Liz, it doesn't. Come on, time to see what this bar is made of."

Chapter Eighteen

Mitch

"YOU CAN JUST LEAVE the serving tray, Viernan. I'll serve our guests," I directed before turning to the three curious faces trained on mine.

"Certainly, sir. Please call if you need anything else."

"Thank you."

I waited until the door clicked shut. "I'm sure you are all wondering why I brought you up here. There is no easy way to say this. My father and Ana were attacked about fifty miles from here."

The room erupted with sound as Tori, David, and Liz started asking questions at once.

"Are they OK?

"What do you mean, attacked?"

"Where are they now?"

I held a hand up and they quieted. "I will tell you everything I know. They were attacked as soon as they reached the home of my father's former colleague. As they approached the front door, they were fired upon. Dad was hit in the chest twice. Thankfully, he was wearing a bulletproof vest. Ana took a graze to the temple, but she reassures me that she is fine.

"How frightening!"

"Do they know why they were being shot at?" David asked.

"Whoever it was didn't want them to enter the house. When police sirens drew near, the shooters ran. Dad and Ana saw the front door was ajar but waited for the police to get there before entering. It's a good thing they did." I sighed, running my hand across the smooth desktop. "The owner of the house was dead."

"I'm so sorry to hear that."

"Oh no!"

"Shit."

"After the police were satisfied they were unlikely suspects, Dad called on some of his own security personnel to ride with him and Ana to the meeting at headquarters. He's worried about us and is sending a detail unit here."

I paused, trying to steel myself before relaying the next bit of information. "Tori, he believes there is a credible risk to Cami, Eric, Barb, and Floyd. If not now, then in the future. We need to call them and put them under our protection. My father has three teams on standby."

"Oh no," she groaned, closing her eyes. She jerked, her eyes popping open as she asked, "Wait, why three?"

"One for Barb and Floyd, one for Cami and Eric, and one for the children."

The room grew quiet as the reality of the threat sunk in. David and I may be used to living with the risks, but the rest of them sure the hell weren't. *Not until you dragged them into this.*

Tori's tortured look was one I knew would haunt my nights. Just the thought of little Jack or Maddie getting caught in the crosshairs of this was incomprehensible. To Tori, it may just be inexcusable.

I didn't have the luxury of worrying about the long-term effects of this on our relationship though. I needed to make good on the promises I had made to keep her and her loved ones safe.

"My father seems to think the hard drives they recovered from the house will contain the information we need to lock up quite a few members of this ring. They are taking them to Jax to see what he and the team can figure out. Once they have what they need, they'll pick up Alfred and Justin on their way back. But this is where all of us will have some hard decisions to make."

My throat constricted and I reached for the shot of whiskey I had poured from my father's collection. Downing it, I continued, "The security team my father is sending to us isn't for protecting us while we are here. He says the house is as close to impenetrable as anyone could hope for."

"Then what will they be here for?" Tori asked, her brows dipping.

"To escort us, should we wish, to an equally secure location while we wait for the danger to pass."

"I'm confused. If we are safe here, why would we want to leave?"

"I suspect because although he feels confident this house could withstand a showdown, this is his sanctuary. Flying bullets and explosives may put a damper on that," I finished with a wry grin.

"B-bullets and explosives?" Tori asked, a loud hiccup escaping. Her eyes widened as she sucked in a deep breath, her eyes avoiding mine.

Cursing inwardly at my insensitivity, I tried to temper my response. "I'm sorry. I spoke out of turn. We don't know if it'll come to that but in our professional experience," nodding to David, "it's not off the table. There is a lot at stake for several high-powered people, Tori."

"Yeah, and they don't tend to go down quietly," David added.

"Where would we go?" Liz asked quietly.

"Another piece of property owned by my father, about thirty minutes away from here. Just as secure but a little more kid-friendly, he assures me."

"Excuse me," Liz exclaimed before abruptly getting up from her chair.

"Liz?" David asked, rising.

Her almond eyes were shining with unshed tears. "It's just a lot to t-take in. I'm sure I'll be fine in a mom—" Her words caught on a sob as she hurried toward the study door.

Tori started to go after her when David laid a hand on her arm. "Do you mind if I go, Tori?"

She searched his face before nodding. "OK, but let me know if she doesn't want—" she stopped.

"To talk to me?" he finished. "Of course."

The grim determination on his face said he wouldn't accept her refusal easily.

The room was silent as Tori and I faced each other.

"Tori, you don't know how sorry I am to have to give you this news."

"You have now put everyone I love at risk," she said, her expression glacial. "I think it's about time you tell me what it is you do for the CIA. Don't you?"

No, my mind yelled. Outwardly, I nodded. "If that's what you need to hear."

"Oh, I think it is."

"I can tell you generalities, but I'm bound by oath and honor to take specifics to my grave, Tori. And we must contact your friends soon."

"Yes, I know," she said pointedly.

In a voice as matter of fact as I could make it, I began what would most likely be the end of us.

Chapter Nineteen

———— ❧ ————

Tori

WATCHING THE HESITANCY EVIDENT from every inch of Mitch, I braced myself for the worst. As he began his story, I was glad for the inner shore-up.

"I met Jax soon after my mom died. I was graduating high school and he was speaking at a career fair set up for seniors. He made the job seem exciting. Special combat training, secret identities, and worldwide travel—what more could an eighteen-year-old want? It was almost too much to turn down, but somehow, I did."

This wasn't what I expected, and I frowned in response as I waited for him to continue.

"My shop teacher had a private woodworking shop and was looking for an apprentice. I had always been fascinated by the detailing and skill involved in making things from different types of wood. Our home had been filled with an oddball assortment of pieces that I know now were from my mother's travels. She had passed them off as yard sale finds." He smiled gently, shaking his head.

"I had a natural skill, something my shop teacher was happy to cultivate. When he offered what was basically a paid internship, I thought I was in heaven."

"I know the feeling."

He had the grace to look uncomfortable. "We can help you get any type of job you want, Tori. I'll see to it."

"I'll hold you to that. For now, you were saying?"

Running his hand through his hair, he continued, "In my first few months, I developed an aptitude for carving. My hands were steady, and I had an eye for symmetry and proportion, my teacher said. He gave me increasingly more intricate designs to replicate before allowing me to create my own. I made everything from wooden pottery and walking sticks, to larger carvings on furniture pieces like armoires, headboards, and—"

"Let me guess, desks?" I interrupted.

"Yes, how did you know?"

"Just a hunch." I was surprised he hadn't noticed but decided to keep the findings to myself. Then, something hit me. "Wait, did you make Professor Cummings's walking cane, by any chance?"

He looked pleased. "Yes. I noticed he was limping when I first met him. As we met regularly for updates about Justin, we grew close. Making him the cane helped take my mind off Ana for a while."

I hid another smile. Now, I was sure of the connection.

"Go on."

"As you know, Ana is a couple years younger than me. She was always better in studies and had skipped a grade, so she only graduated a year behind me. Her senior year, Jax was at her career fair, too. He gave her the same pitch, and she jumped at the offer. When I found out, I made the mistake of telling her I thought it would be too dangerous for her. She signed up the next day."

My heart ached at his forlorn expression. "That still doesn't explain how you ended up here."

"I couldn't leave my baby sister to a life filled with danger without being able to protect her. With my mother gone and my father nowhere in sight, we only had each other. I thanked my teacher-turned-employer goodbye and enlisted right behind Ana. We've served together for nearly two decades," he said with pride.

"Is that normal? Family members working together at the CIA?"

"It happens. The relationship must be kept under wraps though. The fewer vulnerabilities exposed, the better. Most agents keep their real identities hidden even from each other. Only David and Jax know that Ana is my sister. And I would trust them both with our lives."

"If Ana has been at this as long as you have and you're about to retire, why hasn't she?"

"She always said she was a lifer. Before the incident in Brazil, she felt she'd be content in a support position sitting at a desk when her body started to protest active field duty. I'm not sure she feels that way now."

A silence descended. Sitting back, I visually traced the intricate patterns carved into the face of the desk. It was an unusual pattern: a large tree centered about a quarter of the way down, its branches spidering out toward each end of the desk front. A couple dozen birds were hidden among them, each created with exquisite detail. *Are they crows?* I jolted as Mitch's voice broke through my concentration.

"Ana was a natural in her training. All of it. It was obvious to everyone she would make an excellent field officer. I knew I needed to concentrate on my own training if I hoped to remain near her. I thought fighting would be my biggest weak spot; I was never one for needless violence. So, I focused on speed, efficiency, and strength. The hard work paid off and I excelled in combat training. However, there are many skills a field officer must possess. It wasn't long before I realized I was making a weaker showing in a few areas than my fellow recruits. I was afraid of being delayed or worse yet, relegated to a desk position. One of our instructors mentioned a special position in the agency that was often sent on team-led assignments. He thought my natural assets, as he called them, would give me an advantage."

I knew all too well what those natural assets were. My hands clenched and I focused on a stack of books behind Logan's head while he continued.

"Often, our gains are made by recruiting everyday people surrounding our targets. They just need to have access to the information, and we take it from there. My job has been to find out what their motivators are: fear, insecurities, greed, or power. I then use them to develop a working relationship. The assets supply me with information, and I give them something they want in return."

"What information were you hoping to get from me?" I asked stoically, as if my heart wasn't shattering into a thousand pieces.

"Y-you weren't there for information," he answered, sounding uncharacteristically hesitant. "You see, Ana had already gathered the information she thought we needed from them. Someone caught on before she could get it to us, forcing her into hiding. We still don't know everyone involved in this, so we didn't know who we could trust to get her out. We have one agent out there, but he may be under surveillance. It was too risky. I waited six months to lead a rescue mission. Then, I had two weeks to find someone to take to Brazil that would be positioned to both act as a decoy and to allow us entry if we needed further access to the embassy. But mainly, you were there to cause a speck of worry for whoever was involved. I swear Tori, they would have found nothing because we told you nothing. You would have simply gotten the internship and adventure I promised."

The pronouncement had an odd effect. I realized that the image of Professor Mitch Logan was finally ruined for me. Logan Ravenschall, a CIA agent who used the codename of "Raven" was firmly in its place. It was an unsettling feeling and a part of me mourned the loss.

"Pardon me for not feeling confident that 'they would have found nothing' would have kept me and Sebastian safe. I realize you didn't know Liz and Drake were coming when we first met, but was Sebastian in your original plan, too?"

"No. Neither the agency nor I wanted to involve children."

"Then why did you allow it later?" I hated the catch in my voice.

I watched as Logan rose and walked around the desk. Turning the other chair to face me, he sat down, his long legs on either side of mine. His eyes searched my face for a moment before answering. "The night I walked out of your house after we first shared information about our private lives, I was attacked."

My mouth opened; an exclamation of dismay frozen inside. Sucking in a deep breath, I finally managed, "By whom? Are you alright? Clearly, you survived, but why didn't I know?"

He laid a hand on my wrist, squeezing before letting go. "It's fine, Tori. I'm fine. I was blindsided in a moment of distraction. I can't tell you all of it, but I'll just say that the incident was the first time I realized I had to keep you both with me at all times. It was the only way I could think to keep you safe without blowing the entire mission. I still needed to rescue Ana, but Mikaela presented a complication that I had to neutralize as quickly as possible."

"Mikaela? As in that awful excuse of a human being that tried to steal the dress I was wearing and then later showed up at dinner?"

"Yes. I told you we had history. What I didn't tell you is that it was related to the agency."

"So, she was one of the other unwitting women you seduced for something the CIA wanted?" The bitterness sounded vitriolic, even to me. Realizing I was feeling a twinge of sympathy for the disdainful beauty, my anger reached boiling point.

"Yes. And I will not hide behind any more lies or half-truths when there is another way. You deserve to know as much of the truth as I can share. There have been many women I've seduced over the course of my career, Tori. High-ranking mistresses, actresses, even the wives of powerful men. I have always been safe about it. And other than Mikaela Blanc, I have always obtained the information we needed."

The damning words sat in the still air of the study with the finality of a death-row inmates failed last pardon. And even though the words themselves sounded arrogant, the manner he relayed them in did not.

I was left to sit in all my righteous outrage, feeling confident that I would never be able to do, once, what Logan had made a career of doing. But the truth was—a tiny voice in my head pointed out—he'd made the ultimate sacrifice to keep someone he loved safe. This had not been his first choice of career. He had learned new skills while pushing his limitations and for what? To follow his baby sister into the dangerous career she had chosen. Obviously, by any means necessary. Swallowing down the need to lash out at him, I merely asked, "May I ask why Mikaela proved to be the exception?"

"Because I couldn't find one redeeming thing about her. Even if I could have convinced her to turn on her father, I had zero confidence that she would have remained loyal to our deal if she thought her father could offer her more."

"So, it was her father you were after."

"Yes. And although I can't tell you why, I can tell you he's a bad character."

"Well, I doubt I'll ever run into him, so I'll take your word for it."

Logan looked away, shifting his legs. "Actually, you already have," he stated before turning to meet my gaze once more. "That was who we took into custody at the airport."

I was eye-locked with him so I knew he saw the moment I realized who he was talking about. He also witnessed the second my brain played back the picture of Mikaela Blanc's father kneeling down to talk to Sebastian, rustling his hair as if in affection.

Wisely, Logan sat back, his eyes guarded.

I hadn't felt this much anger toward someone since Sean missed Sebastian's birthday to get high. Even his preventable death had filled me with more sadness than anger. But now, I was shaking with the need to let out red-hot rage. The desire for preservation was all that remained of my self-control. I still needed this man's protection, along with the considerable amount of resources his father and the agency could provide. *Speaking of protection...*

With herculean effort, I kept my tone flat while responding "I appreciate your honesty and for telling me more than your agency probably wants an outsider to know about its operations. I believe it's best if I contact Cami and Barb now, as you suggested. None of them deserves the mess we're about to subject them to, but it's too late to sit around lamenting that, now. As to where we should wait this out, where do you feel we will be the safest? It appears I must place my trust in you for the time being."

He flinched at my last statement but nodded his head. "Do you want me to explain it to them or do you prefer to speak with them first?"

Digging out my phone, I found Barb's number. "Let me break it to them and you can do as much damage control as possible." My heart was thumping hard and fast in my chest and I took a deep, relaxing breath before responding to Barb's greeting.

Chapter Twenty

―――――― ❧ ――――――

~~Mitch~~ Logan

CLOSING THE DOUBLE DOORS, I turned to watch Tori's retreating figure head toward the east wing of the house. The calls I had just made weighed heavily on my mind and I walked toward the staircase to find solace in my room.

Barb and Floyd had taken the addition of a security team on their property in stride. I imagined it was an unintended consequence of having dealt with the erratic behavior of their son as he battled his addiction. Not much surprised them. Cami, on the other hand…

"You put two of my friends, and now my family, in danger. You lied to my face when I asked you about that Mikaela train wreck giving Tori a hard time. And now we are supposed to trust you by allowing strangers to camp out on our property and follow us around to prevent something you can't even be sure would ever happen? Are you insane?"

I had looked up to see Tori's lips twitching before she caught my stare and moved further away.

Sighing, I went for the hard tacks I usually reserved for interrogations. "Yes, I did. No, I didn't, at least not completely. And yes, I do. The alternative at this point is to do nothing and hope that the CIA is wrong, and your family goes about their business until someone gets hurt and you can despise me even more because I could have prevented it and didn't."

The silence was charged even through the phone.

Eric's voice cut in a second later. "Mitch—err, I'm not sure what to call you. I'm sorry about my wife's outburst. She's very protective of her loved ones as am I. We understand that you were just doing your job"— a feminine snort sounds faintly over the last word— "and now you are offering your protection out of an abundance of precaution. However, Cami and I feel confident that our own security can provide satisfactory protection."

"Mitch is fine for now. And you're wrong, Eric." I cut through. "My father watched a former CIA officer involved in this gunned down after his wife and 3-month old child were murdered in front of him. These aren't your normal bad guys. They are mercenaries and assassins hired to do one thing and one thing only: eliminate any threats. Accept my father's offer, please." Softening my tone, I added, "I didn't know how deep this went before I brought you all into it. I'm sorry, Eric. For all of it. If anything happens to any one of you, I'll never forgive myself. Let me try to make it right."

"I'm sorry, can you give me a moment, please?" Eric asked before silence greeted me.

Not even the sound of his breathing came through the line and I wondered briefly if he'd hung up. I wouldn't blame him, but I'd keep calling until he agreed to the extra security. Not only did I not want something to happen to any of them for their own sakes, but also for Tori's. She was unlikely to forgive me for any of the current circumstances, as they were.

I was relieved when he returned to the call. "OK, we can shelter them in the guesthouse, and they can coordinate with our head of security, Marcus. I'll text Tori his number. Have your father's team call him to arrange everything."

My head had fallen back as I thanked the heavens for his answer. "Excellent. Thank you, Eric."

"I'm doing it for the protection of my family, not for you," was his cool reply.

"I understand and I think you made the best decision."

"Mm. I'm curious about one thing, though, and I expect an honest answer. There should be no reason for you to lie about this, at least."

Grimacing, I had replied, "I'll answer as honestly and thoroughly as I can."

"Do you have feelings for Tori or was that all a part of your MO?"

Looking at Tori reading the titles of books behind my father's desk, I had tried to think of a discreet way to answer. "That's a bit hard to answer right now."

"Ah. Then just answer yes or no."

"Yes. And then some."

"Then I pity you," Eric said, his amusement evident by his tone. *'Oh, you will when I'm done with him!'* was Cami's faint reply. "You've got an impossible job ahead of you if you hope to carve out a future with her now."

133

"Thanks, I'm well aware," I replied dryly. Catching Tori's look again, I drawled, "Good thing I'm used to overcoming impossible odds."

I had ended the call with Eric's chuckle sounding in my ear.

I was snapped back to the present by the sound of approaching footsteps. Pausing, I swung around to find David walking toward me, an uncharacteristic frown on his face.

"How is Liz?"

"That's what I came to talk to you about. Got a minute?"

"Sure. We can duck into my room." Walking to the end of the hall, I entered the last door, gesturing for David to precede me.

I moved to the far wall, forcing the curtain back to expose the view of the gardens I hadn't had time to explore.

David pulled out the sturdiest chair and sat down, facing me. "I'd like to take Liz and Drake somewhere I don't think anyone will ever think to look for them."

Surprised, I considered the risks of being down a man before we even reached the safe house my father had waiting. Then I realized this meant I'd have Sebastian and Tori to myself. Knowing David was more than up to the task of keeping Liz and Drake safe, I warned him, "I'm OK with it but are you sure she will be?"

"This whole thing has really freaked her out. I convinced her that splitting the targets up will make it harder to pin any one of us down."

"It'll also make it harder for the extra manpower my father has assigned to us," I pointed out. "Where are you taking her?"

"To my mother's childhood home, in Copperopolis. It sits on Lake Tulloch. Usually, my dad rents it out, but it's been going through some renovations. They should be nearly done, and I can rent it until we receive word that it's safe to return the ladies."

"If we receive word. You know there are no guarantees at this point."

"Yeah, I know. I have to believe that all this will come to an end at some point. I've never heard of an investigation lasting so long."

"I imagine there have been a lot of players involved. All we can hope for is that the information Ana has collected is detailed…and current."

He nodded grimly. "What about you and Tori? You're still in one piece so it looks like the Emerald Raven hasn't completely lost his touch."

"Ach. Ana still has a lot of making up to do for that abysmal nickname."

"It's better than the one my brother gave me," he shrugged.

At my inquisitive look, he grinned. "No way am I giving you that kind of ammo."

"I've seen you in enough compromising positions over the years. I don't need a nickname from what I'm sure were more innocent times. Isn't that right, Twigs & Berries?

"Hey! I doubt even you would have been able to tell she was a he," he defended himself while rising from the chair.

Laughing, I instructed him to leave the address of the lake house before showing him the door.

Left alone finally, I removed my shoes before lying on the king size bed. The plush pillowtop surrounded me like a woman's embrace. Thoughts of Tori tossed around my brain as I considered my best course of action. Despite my bravado on the phone with Eric, I was on uneven ground. There was no ready plan to help ease the hopelessness seeping in.

I must accept that even if I saved the girl, I may have still lost her.

Chapter Twenty-One

───── ❧ ─────

Tori

"**M**OM, LOOK! THIS FISH only has one flipper!"

Smiling at his excitement, I leaned close to the glass. "You're right, bud. Good eye! He must have gotten it caught in something." Then it hit me, Sebastian had just pronounced the 'r' in 'flipper.'

These years are going by too fast, I thought sadly.

"Sebastian, look at this snail!"

"Cool! This one is bigger!"

"Liz, are you alright?" I asked softly as soon as the boys moved to the other side of the room to get a better look at the bright coral.

She stared into the aquarium, the blue-green glow of the glass wall casting much of her features in shadows.

"Ever since Alex died, I've played it safe. I focused on Drake and making sure he didn't doubt for one moment that he was loved. Then we moved here and met you and Sebastian," she turned to me with a smile.

"And suddenly, your life is filled with more adventure than you could hope for," I finished, my heart aching for the security that I was partly responsible for taking from her.

Her eyes widened. "No, that's not what I meant. Meeting you feels like an awakening. I thought I was doing the right thing for Drake by staying home and focusing just on him. Now, I realize that I've been depriving him of experiences that I, alone, cannot give him."

"I'm flattered but I think you're underselling yourself. I'm sure Drake would be perfectly content if it remains just the two of you."

"Content, yes. Happy, though? Challenged and excited by more than videogames or the occasional treat? I'm not so sure." She turned to watch the boys as they contorted their mouths into a semblance of a fish's.

We both smiled at the sight.

"And would David have something to do with this recent soul-searching?"

Her head dipped for a second before it jerked up, her chin jutting forward. "He does. I've decided it's time to stop being afraid of love. Even though things didn't work out between us last time, he seems different now. Neither of us are the same people we were back then, really, and I think we have as good a chance as anyone of finding happiness with each other."

This was one of the longest speeches I had ever heard from Liz and I hurried to mask my incredulous expression. "I couldn't agree more, Liz.

I hope you and David make it this time. If there is anything I can do to help make this happen, let me know."

"Actually, there is something I'd like to get your blessing on."

"I'm no heavenly being," I laughed, "but I'll see what I can do. What is it?"

"Don't be mad that I'm not going to go to the safe house with you," she rushed out, shocking me into silence. "David asked if he could take Drake and I to a lake house his family owns. It's only an hour away and he says it's somewhere no one would ever think to look for us. I think he's right, Tori, and I told him we would come with him."

Reeling, I stared at the exotic fish swimming by without really seeing them. If Liz went with David, then it would mean Sebastian and I would be in a house alone, with Logan. My stomach tightened before I chastised myself for cowardice. *You can handle anything he dishes out, Tori.* Besides, he could no longer get away with the lies he was so used to hiding behind.

He managed your friends pretty well, a devilish voice reminded me. Except for Cami, of course. But I knew her anger sprang from hurt. She hated to be lied to more than anything else. I had little doubt Logan could bring her around to his side eventually. Especially since it sounded like Eric had forgiven him, if the conversation on the phone was any indication. Even though I had walked away in the study when Cami had first come on the line, I remained close enough to catch most of his chat with Eric.

When he admitted to caring for me, my heart had somersaulted. But he still had a way to go to earn back my trust. I just had to keep my body from betraying my brain.

139

Shored up, I gave Liz a wink, taking her delicate hands in mine. "Not only am I not going to be mad, I'm going to be as giddy as the two burgeoning mermen before us!"

Returning my grin, she hugged me tightly. "Thank you. I've never been so terrified in my life."

"Well then, rest assured you're making the right choice. Only the things that mean the most to us have the power to inspire terror at the thought of losing them."

"I don't know, losing my virginity was one of the scariest moments of my teenage years. When it was gone, I couldn't have cared less."

Laughing outright, I feigned shock, "Liz, I think it's good you're getting some distance from us. Clearly, I've become a bad influence on you."

With an indelicate snort, she replied "I think I've just finally learned that even a simple woman needs a little excitement in her life."

"I couldn't agree with you more. And since we still have to tell Drake and Sebastian we are separating them, we're about to get all the excitement we need."

Groaning, she followed me to gather the boys.

***

Packing the last of Sebastian's clothes and straightening, I took my phone out to check the time. Eight o'clock. It was time to meet everyone downstairs.

Taking one last look out the window into the darkness, I saw two black limousines and two luxury SUVs parked in a neat line outside the house. Logan had told us after dinner that they were each the equivalent of an armored truck, only sleeker. He also gave us an update on Ana and his father, letting us know that the meeting at the agency went well and they had already begun pulling useful information from the hard drive they had recovered. He outlined our removal to the new locations, saying his father felt us leaving at night would offer the best protection.

The security detail had shown up shortly after and their arrival bolstered Logan and David's moods. While Mrs. H had fed the men in shifts, we had gone downstairs in high spirits to view the comedy Liz and I had picked out.

Pulling the curtains closed, I turned to take in the richness of the room's décor once more. I grabbed the two small bags I had asked the men who came to collect our things to leave, wondering what our intended destination would look like. Perhaps it'd be too much to expect that the house included a pool or other suitable body of water to swim in.

Clearly, I had grown spoiled in my brief time here.

"Tori, do you need help with anything else?" Logan asked from outside the doorway.

"I've just got two small bags and I can get those," I replied before swinging the door open. "Is Sebastian OK?"

"Yes, he's being fawned over by the house staff. It seems he and Drake have made quite a few fans here in a short time."

"You know better than most that a little masculine charm can go a long way," I teased.

"While feminine charm can help you reach the heights of heaven…or bowels of hell," he grinned.

The sight of him leaning against the doorframe, muscular arms peeking from the sleeves of his navy-blue shirt, was discomfiting. Dragging a shaky breath in, I cursed inwardly as I dropped one of the bags.

We both leaned down to grab it, our heads narrowly missing one another. Looking into his eyes, I was mesmerized by their descent until his lips touched mine. I dropped the other bag, moaning in approval as Logan pulled me upright. His hands moved through my hair, cradling my head as his lips staked their claim.

The smell of him was enough to send my arousal into a fervor. A new cologne with hints of sweet bergamot and heady sandalwood mixed with his own scent.

I inhaled deeply, breaking off our kiss to bury my face in his neck. "Logan, we have to go," I managed through hitched breaths. "They are all waiting."

"Mmhm." His mouth laid a series of fires everywhere it touched my skin. Moving his hands down my nape and sliding them down my arms, he pulled me in for a final chaste kiss.

"You're right, it's time to go. But I insist on taking these."

Sighing, I gave in with an ungracious "Fine, since you insist."

Chuckling, he tossed both bags in one arm and stepped aside, gesturing for me to exit first.

Chapter Twenty-Two

~

Logan

WATCHING SEBASTIAN'S HEAD BOUNCE softly against Tori's shoulder, I contemplated his easy acceptance of the past few days' events. Other than the five minutes of protesting and cajoling from him and Drake after we'd told them we would soon be going our separate ways, he seemed to take the disruptive events in stride.

I slid my eyes over Tori's resting features, acknowledging that she deserved credit for a good part of that. The house amenities and staff may have provided excellent distractions, but it was Sebastian's confidence in knowing he was loved that allowed him to enjoy them without a care. And that came from Tori alone.

Saying goodbye to my father's house had been surprisingly difficult. I still wasn't sure how I felt about him not being there to send us off, especially knowing he was injured. Overall, my feelings for him were in a vortex, churning with impressions of the past and present.

It was safe to say he wasn't the villain I had grown up believing him to be.

Who knows, maybe we will achieve some semblance of a family now that Ana is back.

"It won't be long, now, sir," a voice sounded from the divider's speaker.

"OK, thank you," I returned.

That was either Steve or Nick, I thought with a grin, recalling Tori's comment when the twins had introduced themselves.

"Well, your names will be easy to remember, at least," she had smiled up at them. "I love Stevie Nicks."

"Our mother did as well, ma'am," Steve had beamed back.

The men were both around 6'4" and nearly identical in coloring and features. One difference I had noted was Steve's large diamond stud in one ear that stood out against his short, dark hair. Less noticeable but still helpful for distinguishing one from the other, Nick's hair was a couple of inches longer on the sides and back than his brothers.

"Better you than me," David had whispered when the men had gone up to get our luggage. "Personally, I wouldn't want those two holed up around my girl for months. Better keep an eye out."

Despite the faint alarm his words brought, I had chuckled, "That's the difference between us older men and you young bucks: we know how to keep our ladies too happy to look elsewhere."

"OK, grandpa, but her long-term happiness isn't what those young'uns would appeal to, if you catch my drift."

I had merely rolled my eyes as he turned toward Liz and Drake, laughing along the way.

As the men assigned to David, Liz, and Drake had walked toward the front door carrying the trio's belongings, it appeared Fortune had smiled on David. Both men assigned to him were older, with none of the boyish good looks that Steve and Nick had been blessed with.

Shaking my head, I had turned to see Mrs. H enveloping Sebastian in a spirited hug, rocking him back and forth before pulling back to lay a loud kiss upon his head. Grinning at his embarrassed look, I searched for Tori among the shifting occupants of the entranceway.

My frown had stopped Viernan's trek to open the front door for Steve and Nick as they returned, their arms loaded with bags, to inquire about Tori's location. That was when I discovered she was still in her room, packing the last of her and Sebastian's things.

She had looked so melancholy when the door swung open, I was determined to uplift her mood. Our kiss showed a promise I hadn't dared to believe in since our latest fallout.

Tori's initial sadness was something I understood since I felt the same as the time of our departure had drawn nearer. I hoped the house we were moving to would prove as comfortable as this one. Remembering the graceful movements of her body in the pool, I also hoped it would provide somewhere she could enjoy a good swim in.

And, perhaps, a jacuzzi tub? I threw out to the universe.

Looking out the window of the limo, I could just make out a set of palatial gates as we came to a stop at a guard station. Two guards stood at attention, one holding something just out of our sight. I assumed it was a gun and I sent a quick thank you to the sky that my father was the man he was today.

I needed to coordinate with his security team before I was satisfied everything has been done to ensure Tori and Sebastian's safety, but this was a good start. Glancing up at the cameras partially hidden in the trees flanking each gatepost, I nodded my head. *Yes, a very good start indeed.*

The guard standing closest to the window exchanged a few words with Steve before checking a tablet-like device.

A stirring from the back of the car distracted me and I turned to see Tori rubbing her hand across her mouth. The movement jostled Sebastian, who let out a loud yawn.

"Are we there yet?" he asked sleepily.

"Yes, bud. We're here. You woke up at the perfect time."

Tori leaned her head close to the glass and I turned to do the same.

We traveled down a paved driveway when a large stone wall and another set of gates appeared. Where the first were the perfect mix of style and functionality, these were clearly intended for one purpose: to keep unwanted visitors out.

The limo stopped a foot away from a large post that I assumed housed an electronic checkpoint of some kind.

I watched as Nick got out of the passenger side and walked up to it. He was holding a tablet similar to the one the guard had used as his fingers moved quickly over the front of the post. Bending down, he peered at the center of it at eye level, his body stiff. He straightened and nodded to Steve before waving to the SUV behind us.

The solid gates opened and we inched forward as the SUV holding three other security personnel drove past.

Steve pulled up so close to the post, his side mirror missed it with millimeters to spare.

The gates glided back together, their solid steel surface a clear message of strength and warning.

Rolling down his window, Steve took the tablet from Nick before turning back. At this closer view, I was able to see a keypad and screen as Steve keyed in a code. The unmistakable lines of an eye reader laser emitted from the black screen as he leaned out of the car, holding his body still during the scan.

The gate rolled open once more.

Nick's voice sounded from the speaker. "Sir, Mr. Ravenschall instructed us to have you scanned into the system, as well. Would you like to do that now or wait until the morning?"

"I'll wait until morning, Nick, thank you. I'm sure we're in good hands tonight." It wasn't easy to leave things to others, but I could admit that I trusted my father's choices when it came to security. Blaming him for my mother's death had been a blind kick, since at the time, he hadn't even thought up the billion-dollar security company he now owned and operated. Besides, if the world's defense and intelligence agencies trusted in his products and services, then I could, too.

We passed through the gates and around a bend of trees before we caught sight of our sanctuary. The front of the two-story brick house was well lit, offering a warm welcome.

As the entirety of it was revealed past the towering fountain bubbling in the center of the circular driveway, I let out a whistle. Tori gasped and even Sebastian mustered a sleepy "Wow, it looks like a mansion!"

"That's because it is, Sebastian," Tori sighed, rubbing her hands distractedly through his hair. "Your dad doesn't do 'small,' does he?"

"Apparently not." I couldn't keep the worry out of my voice, and she swung her head to pin me with a questioning look.

I shook my head and nodded toward Sebastian. 'Later' I mouthed.

Her brows dipped in response before she turned back to the window. The limo stopped in front of the entrance doors, where three figures were lined up outside of it. The first, and tallest of them, reached for the door handle.

"Welcome, Mr. Logan. I'm Mr. Brander, your butler." He stepped back, allowing me to exit.

"It's a pleasure, Mr. Brander." Turning to offer a hand to Tori, I was left holding onto nothing. Leaning into the limo, I saw her perched on the edge of the seat, her forehead pinched in concentration as she prodded Sebastian forward.

"Do you need a hand?" I asked, hiding a smile.

"I'm alright but Sebastian may need one," she said, watching in concern as Sebastian's legs wobbled. "I don't think his legs are cooperating."

"Ah. No worries. Sebastian, I've got you, bud." Reaching in, I tucked an arm under his legs while supporting his back with the other. He was a light bundle, unresisting in his exhaustion.

Nodding to the car and catching Mr. Brander's eye, I directed, "Please help Ms. McKinley out."

"Of course."

I was happy to see him handling her with care before closing the limo's door.

"Welcome, Ms. McKinley. I'm Mr. Brander. This is Mrs. Lightwell, our housekeeper, and her niece, Miss Hutchins."

"It's a pleasure to meet you all. I'm so sorry if we've kept you up later than usual. We'll be happy to retire for the night if you can show us up to our rooms."

"Mrs. Lightwell and Miss Hutchins would be delighted to. I'll have a few of the staff take your things up."

Mrs. Lightwell moved forward, and her grey curls bounced with an energy that matched the vivacity of her sparkling eyes.

"It's a pleasure to have you home, sir. We've heard so much about you," she smiled widely. "But I can see this young man needs a comfortable bed. You can follow us up to your rooms. We've put all three of you on the top floor of the west wing of the house, where it will be private for you."

As she turned to make her way into the house, her niece waited with a polite smile that nonetheless looked strained around the edges. She pivoted on her heel, about to follow behind Mrs. Lightwell when the light illuminated her young face.

Behind me, Tori's voice rung out with the same word playing in my mind. "Summer?"

Chapter Twenty-Three

―❧―

Tori

GUILT WAS MIXED WITH relief on the petite redhead's face as she smiled up at us. "I was wondering if you'd recognize me!" she said, beaming.

A glance at Logan showed a similar look of astonishment on his face. Too tired to pursue the load of questions now taking up headspace, I sent him a warning look before answering her.

"It's nice to see you again, Summer. Of course, we recognize you. Your hair is a little shorter, but otherwise, you look exactly the same from the last time we met. I'm sure we both look forward to hearing how you ended up here. For now, I think it's best to give Mr. Logan's arms a rest by helping us get Sebastian into bed."

"Oh, sorry. Of course! Follow me!"

Even though I had warned Logan against questioning Summer, I admitted I was eager to hear how she went from working for him at the university to here, at the house he was using as a safe haven.

Stepping into the foyer, I noticed the air conditioning first. The cool air felt heavenly after standing outside, even for the few minutes we were out there. Wiping the beads of sweat from my forehead, I looked around, trying to get a feel for the layout of the house.

In addition to the welcome coolness of the home's temperature, the décor enticed with sunny warmth and comfort. Dark and auburn wood pieces mixed with warm beige, soft white, and lemon-yellow textiles.

In the living room, there were enough throw pillows adorning two inviting couches to make even me content with their numbers. My heels played an eclectic beat as they click-clacked and then grew silent across the wood, tile, and throw-rug covered floors.

Similar landscapes to those in Mr. Ravenschall's main home were sprinkled throughout the check-patterned hallway we walked down next. They were interspersed with portraits and still life paintings, which I intended on taking a longer look at tomorrow.

Logan seemed to agree, as a particular portrait grabbed his attention. He faltered before turning to face forward, rearranging Sebastian in his arms as he started up the stairs.

I only caught a glimpse of the painting, but I got the impression of a blonde-haired woman with vivid green eyes. Possibly his mother, judging from her eyes and his reaction.

It was obvious that Logan's father had never gotten over the loss of his wife. The thought saddened me, as did the amount of time that he had missed with Ana and Logan. Not that they had had it any easier.

Becoming motherless at such young ages must have been excruciating without even a father's love to fall back on.

I shut out the dark thoughts of my own upbringing.

Following behind Logan, I admired the look of the curved railing, its dark finish a contrast to the white spindles supporting it. It was a classic look I'd always admired. In fact, what I'd seen of the house was as close to my dreams of a family home as I'd been able to visualize.

I reached the top floor and Mrs. Lightwell was standing to the side of a doorway Logan and Sebastian disappeared into. She beamed as I approached. "This is his room, ma'am. Yours is right across from him," she whispered, gesturing to the open door across the hall.

My heart flipped at the scene in Sebastian's bedroom. Logan had tucked him under the covers and was removing his last shoe, dropping it gently on the dark rug. Sebastian gave a low groan before flipping onto his side.

Logan looked up, catching my tender look before I could mask it. Ignoring him, I entered the room, stopping to run my fingers gently through Sebastian's hair.

"Goodnight, bud," I whispered. He moved further under the blanket, murmuring unintelligibly.

I spotted his bookbag hanging from the back of a chair. Unzipping it carefully, I pulled out the Mandalorian 'Child' doll from its expected spot. The half plastic, half plush doll had become a favorite since he'd opened it on his last birthday. I had scolded Barb & Floyd for the expense but found myself indebted to them as it became a constant source of comfort for Sebastian.

Contented I had provided as much normality as I could, I followed Logan out of the room.

I closed the door, pausing in front of the temptation in male form. Aware of Mrs. Lightwell's watchful eye, I nodded brusquely. "Thank you for your help. I think it's best if I turn in, too. I'll see you in the morning."

Turning to the housekeeper, I added, "Goodnight, Mrs. Lightwell."

Logan nodded. "Goodnight, Tori."

"Goodnight, ma'am."

Just then, Summer exited my room, her expression as warm and open as when I first met her. "OK, Ms. McKinley, everything is ready for you. I've drawn you a bath, too. I hope that's alright?"

Her look was so earnest, I swallowed a groan of protest. Attempting a smile, I thanked her before walking into the room and leaning my back against the door as it closed.

My eyes shuttered as I took in deep, steadying breaths. Although we had entered the house under a shroud of darkness, it was easy to see that it offered all the protection Mr. Ravenschall had promised.

Resolute, I commanded my heavy lids to open and was uplifted by what they revealed.

The canopy bed was straight out of an off-road antique shop, the delicate floral design engraved on its canopy echoed in the center of a large armoire. White, plush bedding was softened by crocheted lace and hand-stitched pillowcases that brought out the colors of the floral rug. Hand-painted nightstands flanked the bed and the crystal photo frames reflected the soft light emanating from minimalist lamps. A

French-provincial desk sat in one corner, a bright bouquet of flowers its crowning glory.

Moving through the room, I felt some of the weariness leave me. *Perhaps a bath is in the cards tonight, after all.*

Opening one door, I was in awe at the room-sized closet, equipped with glass-fronted cabinets where someone—Summer, I presumed—had already unpacked the few pairs of shoes I had brought with me. My clothing hung from matching hangers, all neatly spaced and organized by color. In the center of the room, an oversized ottoman provided the perfect place to sit and contemplate the day's outfit. Not that I had any desire to do so, but just to have the option was nice.

The second door was open a few inches, revealing the telltale signs of a bathroom. The glimpse of a large soaking tub was all the encouragement I needed to begin undressing.

Yes, this house will do quite nicely, and not just for the security it offers.

However, contemplating its other obvious virtue, I pondered the dangers that came with it. Namely, that the house offered little haven from the assault a certain inhabitant's presence had on both my senses, and my heart.

Chapter Twenty-Four

❧

Logan

"**T**HANK YOU, JARROD. I can see you run a tight ship here, which is a huge relief to me," I smiled at the security head as he finished his presentation. "There are a few changes we need to make due to the current dangers we are facing, and we will need to make accommodations for the additional security team that came with us. Speaking of which, Steve, Nick, how was your night in the guesthouse?"

"Beats the barracks," Steve quipped.

"Slept like a baby," Nicks grinned before adding, "There are three bedrooms and a fold-up in the living room. Steve and I can take the room with the double beds. We're used to sharing everything."

"Well, not everything, little brother," Steve replied slyly. "Unless you count Erica Stev—"

"Little brother? You beat me into this world by three minutes, Steve, for the last time. And you are forgetting Marjorie Hicks. She didn't think there was anything 'little' about me."

I cleared my throat. "OK, you two, I think we get the point. And thank you." Turning to the three men who had followed us last night, I informed them, "You need to move your things from your room into the guesthouse as soon as this meeting is over. Have any of you eaten?"

As they all shook their heads, their eyes hopeful, I turned to the butler. "Can we offer these young men some sustenance, Mr. Brander?"

He bowed his head before answering. "Certainly, sir. Our cook, Mrs. Meetree, sets mealtimes precisely at seven o'clock, eleven-thirty, and five o'clock. Desserts are brought out at seven and are removed by eight o'clock." He hesitated, "Of course, if you'd prefer to make changes…"

"No, Mr. Brander, we have no wish to interrupt your daily routines. At least, not any more than we must. It seems like an unnecessary and frankly, cruel, alteration to your lives when we are here on a temporary basis."

I wondered at his quick frown, noting the differences between him and Viernan. I have grown fond of the latter but suspected that Mr. Brander was a tougher nut to crack.

Glancing at the wall clock, I noted it was already seven-thirty. "Well, men, I'd say if you want to feed your gullets, you'd best leave now. You can move into the guesthouse afterward. Then I'll meet you outside your quarters at nine-thirty to lay out your duties in more detail."

"Yes, Mr. Logan." "Very good, sir." "You've got it, boss."

As the men filed out, my stomach gave a low growl. *Guess I better get some fuel, too.*

Wondering if anyone had let Tori and Sebastian know about mealtimes, I made a quick detour toward the stairs.

The memory of the jolt I had received in the hallway last night hit me. My feet halted in front of my mother's portrait.

The artist had captured the light of excitement that had never strayed far from her green eyes. They had usually been hidden behind large glasses when we went anywhere outside the house. Now I knew why.

Evelyn Mayfair had loved nothing more than creating possibilities for the hopeless. Whether it was reuniting families torn apart by addiction or connecting orphans with couples desperate to offer them love, my mother was happiest serving others. Her strength had been inspiring when I thought she was just a single mother making the best for her children. Now that I knew what she had had to sacrifice to keep us safe, I saw her as otherworldly.

A child's laughter cut into my thoughts. I gave a quick smile to my mom before turning toward the sound. She would have loved Sebastian's exuberance.

"Can you really shoot it that far?" Sebastian's awestruck voice greeted me as I walked into the dining room. The farm-style table was laden with partially empty plates of food, while the trestle benches dipped from the weight of their occupants.

"I sure can, little man. Maybe your momma will let you come out to watch a little target practice sometime." A shoulder was blocking my view, but I recognized Steve's voice, his tone deeper than his brother's.

"Mommy, can I, please?

"When you're older, Sebastian." Tori's voice brooked no argument, and my smile was lost against the buffet wall.

Piling my plate with some of the bounty Mrs. Meetree had laid out, I turned to catch Sebastian's downcast look at his mother's refusal.

The seat across from his was vacant so I took it, Tori's covert glances making me wish the room had several less occupants.

"Good morning, bud. How are you enjoying the house?"

"I have a Star Wars room!"

"You do?" I frowned at Tori before taking a bite of toast. *What would a man with no young children be doing with a Star Wars themed bedroom in his home?*

"Yes, we are in your father's debt for decorating Sebastian's in a way that makes him feel right at home," Tori said, her pleased smile making the oddness seem perfectly reasonable.

I supposed it did offer a plausible explanation. However, it created the questions of how he knew Sebastian liked Star Wars and when had he realized we would even need the room? Either way, my father was full of surprises.

"I'll tell him the next time I talk to him."

"Thank you. Do you have any idea when that will be?"

"In a couple days. He wanted us to get settled first. He should have some information for us about the data Ana delivered, too."

"I hope it's positive information," Tori said, worrying her lip.

Distracted, I answered, "Me too," before falling into silence. How long we stared at each other was uncertain. 'Long enough' was my guess as Nick, seated to Steve's right, cleared his throat.

"Mr. Logan, have you had time to tour the grounds yet? I've been hearing all about them this morning and think Ms. McKinley and young Sebastian would really enjoy some of the things the estate offers." He grinned, "At least, I know I would have at his age."

Steve scoffed, "Who are you trying to fool? You'd still enjoy it, you overgrown toddler."

"Says my genetically matched 'big' brother."

Tori giggled and Sebastian smiled, darting looks between the two men in bemusement. Their lighthearted banter reminded me of David. I'd yet to hear from him but I wanted to wait until I'd spoken with my father before breaking up his time with Liz and Drake.

Hopefully, whatever news I received would be worth it.

"I'd be happy to do it," a cheerful voice piped in.

Summer. I started to tell her I could manage the tour alone when I noted Nick's expression. He was staring at the pretty redhead like she was the premier exhibit at a show he's been dying to see. "That is very kind of you to offer, Summer. Nick, why don't you come with us so you can learn the layout of the house while Steve moves your things into the guesthouse? Then you can show him around when we're done."

"You're the boss, sir," Steve interrupted, "but I think it'd be better if I were to come with you on the tour and let Nick move our things."

"I appreciate the input, Steve, but I think Nick's youth will make the tour easier for him. You are better suited for the responsible task of moving your things into the guesthouse. As you said yourself, you are older than Nick."

Nick guffawed, slapping his brother on his back while Steve grinned good-naturedly.

"Fair enough. I'll enjoy getting first dibs on the beds." He stood, ignoring Nick's sputtering. "Ms. McKinley, Sebastian. Mr. Logan," he nodded before clasping Nick's shoulder in passing.

Still smiling, I turned to Summer, Nick, and Tori. "Let's see what the house has in store for us, shall we?"

Chapter
Twenty-Five

~

Tori

SEBASTIAN HAD BEEN SITTING up in bed when I entered his room in the morning. "Mom! Look at all the Star Wars stuff!" he had cried, gesturing wildly.

I examined the room, my eyes drawn to the source of the bright morning light. It peeked from behind colorful Star Wars-themed curtains covering two large windows.

The shelves hanging above a kid-sized desk were full of action figures holding lightsabers, some still in their boxes. A Death Star hung from the ceiling by fishing line and a Darth Maul alarm clock sat next to his trundle bed.

While I felt the expense was excessive considering the short time we'd be spending here, I appreciated the joy lighting Sebastian's face.

A plain room would have done very little to ease the anxiousness of a new environment.

"Wow, bud! It looks like your dream room, doesn't it?"

"Yeah, it's cool!"

"OK, but remember we're only here visiting with Mr. Logan for a little while. Maybe we can redo your room when we get home. Would you like that?"

"I guess," he grumbled, pulling at the ears of his baby Yoda lookalike.

"Until then, let's go see what other cool things the house has."

"Like breakfast?" Sebastian asked eagerly, forgetting his pique.

"Especially like breakfast."

We had made getting dressed an Olympic-worthy event, walking into the crowded dining room ten minutes later. It had been easy to find; we simply followed the sounds of laughter until our noses led us the rest of the way.

I couldn't make out the individual scents hanging in the air, but I knew they were something I wanted to get closer to.

Catching sight of a large opening on the benches near Summer, Steve, and Nick, I ushered Sebastian toward it.

Steve noticed us first. "Good morning! I see you two are early risers. It's a good thing, too, because I hear the food goes fast."

"Good morning. I believe it. I didn't know anything could smell as tempting as the food at Mr. Ravenschall's main house, but I do now. Based on smell alone, Mrs. Meetree could keep Mr. Blasson from sliding into complacency."

"Don't tell her that," Summer laughed from her spot across Steve. "She'd be crowing all day. She studied under him and has been trying to outdo him ever since she was brought here."

Nick had struck up a conversation with Sebastian about his room and I turned back to Summer.

"Has she been here long?"

"No, about two months. Quite a few of us came along with her. We weren't sure why until we got word that you and Mr. Logan were coming. It's nice to have someone here to look after."

Hmm. So, Logan's father had been planning this for a couple months? But how? I wonder if Logan knows. To Summer, "And speaking of, thank you so much for that hot bath. I was afraid I'd be too tired to enjoy a good soaking, but it was exactly what I needed."

"I'm so happy you enjoyed it, Ms. McKinley."

"Please, call me Tori."

The hollow pit in my stomach gave way to a persistent gnawing. "I'm going to grab some food before it disappears. Would you mind saving my spot?"

"Not at all. I'll keep an eye on everything," she said, pointedly looking from Nick to Sebastian.

"Nuh uh! Darth Maul is scarier!"

"No way, little man. Darth Sidious blows him out the water."

Laughing, I thanked her before heading to the table and buffet server lined against the back walls.

A few trips later, I set my coffee cup down, being careful to keep it out of Sebastian's range. His arms flailed in excitement as he talked to Nick in between swallows. Steve had given up trying to enter the conversation and contented himself with talking to one of the other security men seated near him.

Summer proved a fountain of information about the area and I was enjoying our conversation until she mentioned Logan.

"I'm surprised there are still so many people in here," she said. "I know the men were in a meeting with Mr. Logan this morning, but I thought they'd just get a quick bite to eat and run. I heard that one—she nodded to Steve—tell the guy next to him they had another meeting with Mr. Logan at 9:30."

"Two meetings in one morning?" I mused aloud. "I wonder what they're about?"

"Security measures for you and your son," she seemed surprised by the question.

Shouldn't the security of my son involve me, as well? I fumed inwardly. I was saved from replying by the arrival of the very man we'd been discussing. Despite my irritation, my heart thumped faster against my ribs at the sight of him.

He exuded casual confidence in a black tee and grey trousers. His dark hair fell across his forehead, drawing attention to the impossible green of his eyes. Forcing myself to turn away, I concentrated on Nick's voice as he bragged about his weapon-wielding capabilities, his eyes darting to a clearly unimpressed Summer.

Hiding the twitching of my mouth behind the oversized mug, I mulled over the best way to show Logan he needed to include me in the decision-making.

Clearly, I was dealing with a man used to doing things his way.

Funny. So was I.

Chapter Twenty-Six

~

Logan

FOLLOWING SUMMER AND NICK into the gardens, I was acutely aware of the woman walking beside me. She looked enchanting in a white summer dress with bits of lace trimming the short-sleeves and hem. The neckline was just low enough to drive my heartbeat thrumming in my ears whenever she stopped to look at the plants.

Willing my attention away, I turned to the lush, panoramic scene. The back of the house was an extraordinary sight: one end devoted to outdoor play while the other offered a peaceful setting to relax in. The play area was equipped with a trampoline pad set level with the ground, something that delighted Sebastian when he first saw it.

Equally appreciative, Tori had let out a contented sigh at the swimming pool, its long length perfect for laps. The surrounding deck was littered with vibrant lounge chairs, a canopied bar, and an outdoor shower. The most surprising find had been a treehouse built inside a manufactured 'tree' that shaded its occupants from the hot sun. It was this that had Nick sharing.

"Steve and I made a treehouse just like this one. Unfortunately for me, it was in a real tree, about twelve feet from the ground."

At our inquisitive looks, he added, "He pushed me out of it when we were twelve."

"That explains a lot," Summer drolled, drawing chuckles from us and a shrug from Nick.

Sobering, I considered the odd addition to the yard. I wasn't sure if my father had bought the property with the kid's room and treehouse included, but if he had, it was odd he hadn't converted the spaces to better suit his bachelor lifestyle. Then again, how well did I know the man? Perhaps he was still hoping for a later-in-life romance that would bring children.

A familiar jolt of anger flared before I tamped it down.

"Mom! Logan! Look at this!" Sebastian called, piercing my thoughts as he leaned down to peer at something.

Following the stone path, we reached him just as he stepped back, revealing a sturdy garden bench with a delicate design. The frame was constructed of scrolled ironwork, while the back support was fashioned from wide wood slats. Bending down to get a closer look, I studied a plaque embedded in the center of the top slat.

"May you rest now, darling Evie," Tori read aloud beside me. "Logan, how sweet. Your father must really have loved your mother."

I straightened, the tightness in my throat making speech impossible.

"Sebastian, do you want to see some fish? There is a really cool pond over there," Summer said, pointing to a corner of the gardens.

"Cool! Mom, can I?" he asked, already walking toward it.

"Of course. We'll be there in a moment." She nodded to Summer, the two sharing a look of understanding.

Nick asked to join them and the three headed off together.

I appreciated the moment we had to ourselves. The constriction eased and I managed a short response. "Yes, I see now that he really did." My anger at the thought of him moving on with another wife, another family, disappeared. It was obvious my father worshipped my mother and had paid dearly for that devotion.

The cloud of uncertainty over what I felt for the man who had missed every milestone of my life lifted. In its place was hope. Maybe we could build a relationship based on the mutual love of my mother. *She would have wanted that*, I admitted, closing my eyes briefly.

"These carved pieces are beautiful, too," Tori continued, sliding her hands over the designs flanking the plaque. "Oh! These look like stargazer lilies!"

Frowning at a tugging memory, I leaned in for a closer look. Impossible. "That's exactly what they are," I told Tori through my shock.

"Look at you with the hidden interests," she teased. "I didn't know you were a flower enthusiast."

"I'm not. It was my mother's favorite flower. I am, however, a woodworker, if you remember." I slid my eyes to hers, catching the moment she put it all together.

"Wait. So, these are your—?"

"Yes, I carved them when I was an apprentice. The man I worked under told me they were for a client. I guess I know which one," I laughed wryly.

She fell silent, her forehead creasing. "Did you notice the designs on your father's desk in his study?"

"I remember admiring the overall look of it but no, I didn't get up close. Why do you ask?"

"During your apprenticeship, did you ever carve a tree with branches that were littered with small birds—maybe crows?"

"Ravens," I corrected her. "I made the piece right after I discovered my father's identity. I threw it away, behind the shop."

It had taken me a while to get confirmation from my mother, but I knew there was a reason why she turned off the security company's commercial every time it—or he—showed up on our screen. I remembered feeling the tension emanating from her each time.

From there, it hadn't been hard to put together the bits of information she had relayed about him—especially the unique color of his eyes—and my hatred had gained a physical identity. She never had to ask me again to change the channel when his smiling face crossed our screen.

The carving had been my sarcastic rendition of the many lives I assumed my father's infidelity had touched.

"Well, it's in your dad's study now."

"I'm not sure how it would end up in my father's house."

"Aren't you?" Tori asked softly. "I think he's been a part of your life for a very long time. In fact, I don't think he's ever left it."

As soon as she voiced the idea, I realized the same thoughts had been pulling at the corners of my mind. Even though I had cleared him of the grievous lack of concern for mom, I hadn't been ready to exonerate him of all wrongdoing. It seemed too tragic a reality to face, of Ana and I longing for a father who lurked in the shadows yearning for the wife and kids he could never have.

A jagged breath escaped and Tori reached for my hands. Her soft skin radiated warmth as her thumbs rubbed across my knuckles. I drank up the sight of her, wanting to feel her curves pressed against mine but respecting the inner struggle I could see in her hazel eyes.

She broke the silence first. "Did I ever tell you stargazer lilies are my favorite flower, too?"

"No, but I'm not surprised. Maybe it was my mother who sent you to me."

She swallowed hard, her eyes softening as she breathed out. "Logan, I—"

"Please, Tori. Give us a chance. I can see you are still holding back. I know I broke your trust, put you in danger, and—"

"Is this supposed to convince me?" she drawled.

"No," I laughed before sobering. "I just want you to know I realize I'm asking for something I have no right to ask you."

"Then why are you, Logan?"

"Because I can't imagine living any other life than one with you in it. It's safe to say the Ravenschall's love hard and true. Let me love you like that. I'll spend a lifetime making sure you never regret it."

She leaned toward me and for one glittering moment, I thought she was going to accept my plea. A guarded look crossed her features and she straightened, letting go of my hands.

"I think we should focus on returning everyone's lives to normal."

Crestfallen but nodding in agreement, I looked past her to where Sebastian and Nick were kneeling over the pond, Summer smiling beside them.

A gentle touch on my cheek soothed me. "And then we'll see what lies between us."

Hope surged and I wanted to swing her in my arms, bedamned to any witnesses. I was about to give into the urge when she took a step back, asking, "Aren't you giving a security meeting this morning?"

Digging out my phone, I cursed. I had three minutes to get to the guesthouse around the other end of the house.

"Yes, unfortunately, I must go. Where will you be in the next hour?"

"Finishing up the security meeting, I suppose."

"What? I'm sorry, Tori, this is just for the—"

"For whom? The men?" she said, her toe tapping on the stone.

"I was going to say security detail. I've asked you to trust me, sweetheart. Can you do that?"

"Trust or not, you will keep us safe. You owe us that," she said matter-of-factly. "But this concerns me as an individual, a friend, and especially, as a mother. I'm involved whether you want me to be or not."

"I don't think that's a good i—"

"If I was Sebastian's father, would you still exclude me?" she demanded.

I could feel my mouth go slack as I stopped to consider her question. In all fairness, she made a damn good point. "OK, but what about Sebastian?"

She grinned before calling out to Summer. The redhead walked up to us, her hair turning to fire in the morning sun. Sebastian skipped behind her, chattering to Nick and then to us about a frog they had seen.

Laughing, Tori turned to Summer as soon as she could cut in, "Summer, I was wondering if you had anything pressing to do for the next hour? Logan and I have some things to discuss and I was hoping you could stay with Sebastian while he enjoys the backyard some more?"

"I'd love to," she smiled through Sebastian's joyous squeals. "I'm not needed back until an hour before lunch." Turning to Sebastian, she reached out her hand, asking, "Do you want to give the trampoline a try?"

"Yeah! Let's go!" he cried before dragging her toward it.

"You sure you don't need me boss?" Nick asked, looking longingly after Summer and Sebastian's departing backs.

Tori answered before I could. "Of course, we do. You're on protection detail for Summer and Sebastian until we return. We know they're in good hands."

Sighing, I nodded my OK.

Nick saluted, "Yes, ma'am!" before running after them.

Tori looked at me with a smug grin. "Problem solved. Lead the way."

"Remind me never to bet against you."

"Oh, you're a smart guy. I doubt I'll need to," she said with a jaunty toss of her hair.

Chapter
Twenty-Seven

~

Tori

WATCHING LOGAN AS HE laid out his plans to reinforce the existing security around the house, I noted his calm and concise way of speaking to the men. They were all focused on him, their attention never wavering. He had the same effect on me, and I suspected, most of the people he'd ever come across. *Go ahead, Tori, admit it. You mean the women he's come across.*

Grimacing, I pushed the inner green-eyed monster aside. Logan was laying out the men's schedules, pairing them up in twos and threes.

"Alright gentlemen, my lady," he smiled at me. "That's it. Any questions?"

"Yeah, boss. Nick wants to know if the cute redhead is spoken for?" Steve smirked as some of the men nudged him.

His lips twitching, Logan tried to adopt a stern expression, failing miserably. "Then Nick can ask Summer himself. Any security-related questions?"

"How about you, Ms. McKinley? Are you spoken for?" The question came from the man who had introduced himself as Pete at the start of the meeting.

The group was quiet as Steve and Jarrod backed slowly away from him.

My eyes flitted from Pete's arrogant grin to Logan's face, gasping at the bottled rage emanating from the man who had just been sharing in Steve's joke.

"Ms. McKinley is under my special protection, Pete. I suggest you, and anyone else entertaining similar thoughts, resign yourselves to that. Immediately," he gritted out, staring each man down.

Not that he got any resistance. Everyone suddenly had something else to look at. If I wasn't so embarrassed, I'd be amused. As it stood, I wanted to run inside and bury my head in a pillow. Well, one part of me did. Another part was stretching and laying across a velvet settee, purring in satisfaction.

"Sorry, Mr. Logan, I meant no disrespect, sir," Pete rushed to explain.

"It's not me you need to apologize to, Pete," Logan stated, his words less clipped.

"I apologize Ms. McKinley. I meant it as a sincere compliment."

"Nothing to forgive, Pete. Thank you." I ignored Logan's searing look. I told him I'd give him a chance, not that it was a done deal. An impish voice prodded me into adding, "And for the record, I took it as a compliment."

I regretted it as soon as I saw the hope blaze in Pete's eyes. I needn't have worried as Logan was quick to close the opening I had unthinkingly created.

"You are very kind, Ms. McKinley, as always. I'm sure Pete understands the difference between a lady being polite and one showing interest. Right, Pete?"

"Of course, sir."

I cringed at the additional censure I had brought on the hapless Pete. Making a hasty retreat, I managed a mumbled response as I turned toward the back of the house.

As I reached several feet away from the assembled group, I heard Steve quip, "Well, we all know where you stand on that particular issue, sir."

A chorus of chuckles followed his words, Logan's rich laughter leading them. "Happy to hear it, Steve. Anything I can do to get us all on the same page."

Steve snorted and I lost any more of the conversation as I hurried my steps.

***

Standing up from the table, I smiled at the rowdy group I had just shared a hearty dinner with. The men had been in good spirits at lunch, but after spending some time together in the guesthouse, they had arrived at dinner in raucous harmony.

The group had taken Sebastian under their collective wing, and he was delighted with the attention. After lunch, those that weren't on security shifts had even joined Logan in teaching him a game of touch football. My heart had swelled watching Logan swoop Sebastian into his arms and swing him after a play.

By the time I laid him down for a nap, he was happy and exhausted. "Mom, I like it here," he said groggily. "Do we have to go home?"

The question had taken me aback. He hadn't even asked that at Logan's father's house.

"Did you have fun today, bud?"

"Yes. Now I have lots of friends."

I blinked back tears at his simple pronouncement. "Yes, honey, now you have lots of friends. How could you not?" I ended on a whisper, words failing me. I had sat on his bed, rubbing his back until his breathing grew even.

Now, after saying goodnight to the table, I ushered a protesting Sebastian upstairs again, this time for a bath. Thinking of the last time he took one in a strange home, I wondered how Liz and Drake were doing. I hadn't heard anything from Liz yet, so I decided to call her while Sebastian was washing up.

Leaving the door open so I could hear him, I hit Liz's contact.

She picked up just as I was ready to end the call.

"Hi, Tori!"

"Hi, Liz. How is everything going?"

"So far, so good. Drake and David are playing pool and I was about to take a bath. How are you and Sebastian?"

"Tired but happy. The property here is beautiful and Sebastian has already charmed all the security guys," I laughed.

"I know what you mean. Earlier, David and our security team played basketball with Drake. I've never seen him so happy to take a nap."

"Same here. They exhaust me just watching them. I'm worried he'll never want to leave."

"Surely he'll prefer the comforts of his own home when it's time to return," she comforted.

Listening to Sebastian's lighthearted play from the bathroom, I bit down on the side of my lip. "I'm beginning to wonder."

Chapter Twenty-Eight

~

Logan

A S TORI AND SEBASTIAN walked out of the dining room, I noticed the immediate change in my mood. Gone was the carefree man determined to set a skittish woman and child at ease. In his place was one wracked with guilt and worry.

What if the evidence Ana collected wasn't enough? Or, they never found all the guilty parties? Was I to consign Tori, Sebastian, and their friends to a life of looking over their shoulders? I had never had to deal with the concern of someone's welfare after I had held up my end of the deal. But Tori hadn't known what she was walking into. She'd expected nothing more than an internship to help her career. While I knew I could guarantee her a good job when this was over, I also knew it'd be insultingly inadequate for the upheaval of her life. Of all their lives.

Steve clapped, breaking through my maudlin thoughts. "Well, gentlemen, Miss Summer, it's time for my shift. You can all sleep well tonight knowing your lives are in my hands."

A grin tugged at the resulting groans.

"I don't know about all that, but I agree, it's time for our shift," Jarrod drawled, standing.

I considered the security head, nodding to him when his eyes settled on mine. I was fortunate to have him as he'd proven to be an invaluable source of information about the workings of the house. That, and a wealth of knowledge on modern security technology.

It was from him that I had learned about the hidden features scattered throughout the property. He had stayed after this morning's meeting to fill me in, away from the others. It was my father's wish that some details remained just between Jarrod and two hand-chosen men. *Well, three now.*

The most impressive bit he shared was that infrared and microwave sensors surrounded the perimeter of the walled portion of the property. Jarrod said they picked up the second a line of light waves was broken and had the built-in capabilities to ignore potential annoyances like wind, rain, and most birds. Coupled with a full range of IP and CCTV cameras, the house deserved the pride that had shone through his voice. It assured me I was providing Tori the maximum amount of protection I could.

Recalling the last conversation with my father, I realized tomorrow's call was lingering in my head like an unwanted guest. Of course, there was a possibility the call would bring good news. At this point, I'd welcome uncertainty over a definitive confirmation the data wasn't worth a damn.

"You look like you could use a drink," Nick's voice cut through. "Summer convinced Brander to give us access to the liquor cabinet in the library. We brought a few bottles to the guesthouse. Some decent vodka, whiskey, schnapps—you interested?"

"He gave you limited access," Summer stressed, glaring at him.

Holding up his hands, his eyes wide, Nick reared back comically. "Woah, little lady, I'm sorry. I meant *limited* access. There, am I forgiven?" His over-the-top remorse broke through Summer's irritation and she rewarded him with a twitch of her lips.

Shaking my head at their flirtations but already feeling lighter, I made a quick decision. "What the hell. A drink sounds like just the tonic I need."

So does sinking into Tori's warmth.

Sighing, "Maybe two."

***

"So, the house used to belong to a drug cartel? That's pretty badass," John, the youngest of the men my father had sent with us asked.

"Yeah, Mr. Branders says Mr. Ravenschall bought it at auction after the property was seized," Summer answered.

Nick leaned forward. "Do they know which cartel family?"

"No. I asked the same thing. He did say it's a disbanded one. So, we don't have to worry about anyone coming to take it back."

"Well, that's good. Now, we just have to worry about some unknown entity trying to take out Ms. McKinley and Sebastian," John retorted.

The room got quiet as all eyes except John's fell on me. Oblivious to the tension, he continued, "It's hard to imagine either of them pissing someone off enough to end up on a hit list, but I guess you never know."

Setting my glass down with a controlled snap, I faced him. "The only thing Tori or Sebastian McKinley did to end up in this mess is to trust in me. You'd do well to keep your mouth shut about things you know nothing about."

"I-I'm sorry, sir. I meant no offense."

Taking a deep breath, my voice devoid of the rage churning inside, I reminded him, "You're employed to protect them, not to understand why. I'm fairly certain Mr. Ravenschall made that clear when he hired you."

Chastised, John dipped his head. "You're right, sir. It won't happen again."

Knowing the exchange had ruined the joviality of our small group, I stood. "Good. Enough said about the matter. I need to check on a few things in the house. Enjoy the rest of your night." Turning to Nick, I managed a grin, "Thanks for the drinks."

"Anytime, boss," he smiled back.

"Goodnight, Mr. Logan," Summer said quietly.

The walk back to the main house was too short to quiet the anger still burning a hole in my gut, so I continued to the gardens instead.

The warm air had just enough breeze to rustle the hair falling against my forehead, doing little to relax the lines it danced across.

My legs led me to the bench dedicated to my mother. Sitting down, I turned to trace the inscription on the plaque. Evie. The nickname made her and my dad's love real to me in ways nothing else had. There was so much I realized now I didn't know about her. It was obvious that whatever she was known by, Evelyn Mayfair to Ana and I, or Evie Ravenschall to Dad, she was well-loved.

"What I want to know, Mom, is what made an agent ignore all her instincts and head out alone to meet someone she clearly knew was dangerous?" The breeze was my only answer as I contemplated the question that had been swirling in my mind ever since my father told me how she had died. It didn't add up. No matter how much she loved my father, she was clearly prepared to live without him in order to keep Ana and I safe. Why would she have risked everything to save him?

I sat lost in my thoughts for a few moments, discarding one theory after another. Then, a picture of another mother opening an envelope with a lock of her son's hair filled my head. Tori had known it was Sebastian's in a split second. Was it possible Mom had also known the lock wasn't her husbands, but her sons?

Letting out a growl of frustration, I leaned forward, cradling my head in my hands. *Would I ever know the whole truth?* Sadly, I admitted to myself, it was unlikely.

Scanning the yard, I watched as Tori stepped out of the back door and made a straight line for the garden. She looked at home among the flowers, like a garden fairy frolicking with wood sprites.

"Hey. Everything OK?" she asked, sitting beside me. "Summer said you might need someone to talk to."

The wind swept her hair forward, partially covering her face. The scents of a dozen flowers I'd never know the names of filled my senses as I pushed back the curtain of hair obscuring her eyes.

"Thanks," she laughed, the sound easing the tension my thoughts had caused.

Still enjoying the smell of her, "You changed your shampoo."

Her smile tilted. "I usually switch between two or three of them. I doubt that is what you came out here to contemplate, though. What's going on? Did your father contact you?"

I shook my head, letting out a frustrated sigh. "No. Nothing yet. We'll know something tomorrow, I'm sure. I admit I'm no expert on the man, but judging by what I've seen, when he lays out a plan, he follows through with it."

"Funny, that's what they're saying about you."

"Who?"

"Some of the guys. They speak in hushed tones, but I catch part of the conversations. I think the ranks are torn between being in awe of you and disbelieving you've done some of the things they've heard. Apparently, your father spread some high praise of you when he hired them."

The revelation threw me off and I examined the growing darkness, focusing on the last bit of light draining from the sky. "Most likely embellished stories. He did it to establish a pecking order. Men like Jarrod aren't going to like an outsider coming in, telling them where to improve upon a system they're in charge of. Not unless that person has already established themselves as an expert—someone worth listening to."

The yard was silent except for the occasional insect calling out a warning.

"And are you?" she asked, her tone deepening into the husky tone that haunted my nights.

Turning toward her, I searched the side of her face not obscured by shadows. "Someone worth listening to?"

"An expert."

Arousal erupted bringing a hyperawareness focused purely on the woman within hands' reach. "I'm not sure which area of expertise you're hoping for—"

"Liar."

Chapter
Twenty-Nine

~≈~

Tori

"**T**ORI, ALTHOUGH I THINK you already know the answer to that question, I'd be happy to give you further demonstration. I'm just not sure now is the best time to pursue it." Logan's voice sounded strained to my ears. There was no evidence of turmoil on his face, however, as he turned to greet someone behind me.

"Sir, I'm sorry to interrupt but Steve said you were asking for me earlier?"

Groaning inwardly at the interruption, I faced the stern countenance of the butler.

"Ah yes, Mr. Brander, I did. I'm sorry he sent you all the way out here. I was just about to escort Ms. McKinley inside and look for you.

I was hoping you could give us both a tour of the rest of the inside of the house."

"Of course, sir. There's only a few bedrooms, the game room, and the workshop left. Oh, and the—" he stopped to dart his eyes between us, clearly hesitant to say whatever it was in front of me.

I caught a tugging at Logan's mouth before he sobered. "Right, understood. Well, if Ms. McKinley is available?"

"I am. Sebastian's in bed and Summer said she'd keep her door open to listen for him. I promised her I wouldn't be longer than a half hour, though."

"It seems we are at your disposal, Mr. Brander. Lead the way." Logan said, rising and offering me his hand.

As the solid warmth closed firmly over my fingers, I let out a sigh. A tour of the house wasn't what I had in mind moments before, but I was curious to see more of our temporary haven.

I moved to release Logan's hand as I turned to follow Mr. Brander. I succeeded only in tugging it an inch as he tightened his grip. His warning look thrilled me more than it should, and I left our hands entwined during the short walk to the house. It reminded me of the first time he had grabbed it.

So much had changed in so little time. I wasn't the same woman who had run out of the restaurant, fleeing from an attraction that scared me with its intensity. And that was before I knew just how dangerous loving Logan Ravenschall would be.

Woah. My foot caught as we reached the pavers outside the back entrance.

Logan steadied me easily, bracing my arm while still holding tightly to my hand. His knotted brow framed the concern that shone from his eyes.

I felt spellbound as time seemed to stop.

We stood just outside the door, the bright lights illuminating his dark hair like a beacon. My fingers answered the invitation, sliding from the safety of his firm grip to glide through feather-soft waves.

His eyes never left mine as Mr. Brander cleared his throat, holding the door open for us.

"We'll be right behind you in a moment, Mr. Brander," Logan said.

"But, sir—"

"Close the door, Brander," he commanded brusquely. Neither of us waited for the agitated snap of the door before leaning in for a fiery kiss.

The heat from Logan's mouth was almost enough to drown out the word shouting from the confines of my head.

Love!

Somehow, the emotion had staked its claim on my heart while I was busy trying to determine why I trusted a man who had lied about his very identity.

The truth is, I acknowledged as his mouth deepened its assault, *his reasons for lying are some of the very things I've come to love about him.*

He was a born protector. A man who believed in loyalty and honor but who would unleash a fury of retribution against anyone who endangered those he cared for. He carried a heavy responsibility in his line of work but shouldered most of its aftereffects on his own. His job was not for the rash and undisciplined, nor the weak.

191

I wasn't sure how long I could hold the interest of a worldly man like Logan, but as he pressed his athletic shape against mine, I realized I was past caring.

A moan of protest echoed in the quiet night as he stepped back, untangling my arms from around his shoulders.

"I know," Logan smiled, reaching out to caress my cheek. "But if we take much longer, I'm afraid Mr. Brander may lock us outside for the night."

Grinning, I nodded. "You're probably right. He's no Viernan, is he?"

He snorted. "Viernan wouldn't have needed to be asked to go inside the first time. We would simply have found ourselves alone with a map of the best spots on the property for a late-night tryst."

"And a cart of delicious treats and something strong to drink at each one, no doubt."

We shared a laugh and lingering look before walking inside.

Mr. Brander's disapproving sniff greeted us.

I managed to keep my quivering lip from betraying my amusement. "We're ready for the tour now, Mr. Brander," I offered an olive branch. "Please excuse our delay."

The beanpole of a man unbent enough to glance toward my general direction. "Of course, ma'am. We'll start with the bedrooms on this floor since the hour is getting late," he said pointedly. "Follow me."

As Mr. Brander turned without waiting for a response, Logan followed directly behind him. Stretching his arms out like a monster of old, he walked woodenly in step with the oblivious butler.

A chortle escaped and I hid it behind a cough as Logan straightened just in time for Mr. Brander's abrupt stop.

"If you need something to drink, ma'am, I can request someone brings you something straightaway," he said stiffly.

"No, thank you, I'm fine. I appreciate your concern, Mr. Brander. It shows you are a man of action," I added, hoping to thaw him a trifle more.

He visibly preened. "Yes, quite. Mr. Ravenschall often notes the same about my attention to his health, if I may be so bold to share."

"My father is a lucky man, Brander," Logan added helpfully.

The inflated butler bowed as if he'd just received a Lifetime Achievement award. "Thank you, sir."

Our much more convivial guide continued his tour, disdaining to add bits of history on some of the more interesting pieces found in the rooms.

Each room was lovelier than the next, but it was the sunny craft room that had me gasping.

"If there were a more perfect room invented, I've never seen it," I whispered reverently.

We were bathed in the diffused light of the setting sun, the benefits of being on the first floor with a large window unobscured by heavy coverings. White lace curtains billowed softly above a long window seat. The tufted cushion was covered in a soft blue and white striped pattern that was reversed on coordinating pillows. Flanking both sides were floor-to-ceiling bookshelves painted a bright white. The sparseness of the collection dotting each shelf made me long to fill them with the boxes of books still packed away at home. There hadn't been enough room to display them all when Sebastian and I had moved into the condo, something I hoped to correct with a bigger place once I finished school.

In the center of the room sat a stationary workspace suitable for any crafting project you could throw at it. Multi-drawered cabinets followed an L-shaped pattern underneath, providing plenty of storage for supplies.

Mr. Bander reached under the worktop and a panel on one end opened to reveal a modern sewing machine. I couldn't contain my "Ohh!" of wonder, and Logan broke his amused silence.

"You could make a lot of doilies in here, huh love?" he teased.

I ignored the quickening of my heart at his endearment. "Absolutely. Just think of all the surfaces at your place I could help save from the wear and tear of your everyday manhandling."

"Manhandling?" his eyebrow rose. Taking a few steps, he leaned toward me until his breath tickled my ear. "I'd like to manhandle someth—" he was cut off by an increasingly impatient Mr. Brander.

"If it suits you both, I'll show you the game room but recommend we leave the workshop until tomorrow. It's around the other side of the house and it's getting late."

"Thank you, Brander. That will suit us just fine. I believe we are both ready to hit the sack as well," Logan drawled, shooting me a wolfish grin.

Incorrigible. An eyeroll was my only answer as we turned to follow our weary guide.

Chapter Thirty

Logan

THE TOUR NOW COMPLETED, I turned to face Brander. A pang of guilt hit as his customary pinched look gave way to pure exhaustion. His age was difficult to ascertain, but he looked close to seventy.

"We appreciate your time, Brander. The house obviously benefits from being under your watchful eye. I'll make sure to say as much to my father."

"Thank you, sir. It was my pleasure. Goodnight Ms. McKinley. Goodnight, sir."

"Goodnight, Mr. Brander."

"Goodnight, Brander."

Tori and I were both silent as we watched the butler disappear down the hall. We had ended the tour in front of the stairway, and I moved to the side, gesturing for Tori to go up first.

As she took the first step, I reached for her hand. "Tori, after you relieve Summer and assuming Sebastian is fast asleep, would you come to my room tonight?"

Her lips curled. "That depends."

"I assure you my intentions are noble. Mostly," I couldn't resist adding.

We both stood there grinning at each other before she nodded soberly. "I'll hold you to that. Mostly." With a wink she turned and sashayed up the stairs.

I was left to enjoy the view, trailing behind her until she disappeared into Sebastian's room.

Stopping in front of Summer's partially open door, I rapped lightly. It swung open a moment later and she appeared, looking even younger than her twenty years in two thick braids and strawberry print pajamas.

"Hi, Mr. Logan.

"Good evening, Summer. I hope I'm not disturbing you."

"Nope. I was just reading and keeping an ear out for Sebastian. Did Ms. McKinley find you?"

"She did. That's part of what I wanted to talk to you about. Thank you for sending her to me. It was very thoughtful."

"No worries. After working with you, I learned a little about your moods. And forgive me for saying so, but it doesn't seem like you have anyone to talk to."

Surprised by her observations, I could only stumble out, "Yes, well, it was kind and I didn't want you to think I didn't notice or appreciate it."

"You're welcome, Mr. Logan. I know you'd do the same for me."

Her open expression was a balm. I hadn't spent a lot of time with the truly good people of the world. *They usually aren't the ones that attract agency notice*, I acknowledged ruefully.

"Of course. And on that note, I'll say that young Nick seems to have developed an interest in you. I believe he's a good chap, but if he ever steps out of line, let me know."

Giggling, she nodded. "I will. But don't worry about me, Mr. Logan. I have five big brothers at home. It's Nick who'll need protecting."

"Good. I'll make sure to mention it to him."

"It probably wouldn't hurt."

"No," I laughed softly. "It definitely wouldn't. I just have one more thing I want to discuss before I leave you to your reading."

"Sure, what is it?"

"Did you work for my father before or after you worked with me?"

Her eyes widened but she answered gamely. "Before. I've been with Mr. Ravenschall since I was fresh out of high school. My aunt has known him a lot longer."

"OK, thank you. You made an excellent front desk clerk. I am grateful you were sent to me, either way."

"Thank you, Mr. Logan."

"You're welcome. Goodnight, Summer."

"Goodnight, sir."

A slight movement caught my attention. Tori was closing Sebastian's door and looked curiously at me as she approached.

"Summer and I were just saying goodnight," I told her, deliberately leaving out any details.

She narrowed her eyes before turning a shoulder to me. "He's out like a light. Thanks for keeping an ear out for him, Summer."

"You're welcome, Ms. McKinley. It was no trouble at all."

"And please, call me Tori. I think our friendship warrants the use of first names, don't you?"

Summer's face lit up the dim hall. "Yes, ma'am—sorry, Tori! I do. Well, have a goodnight."

"You, too."

I waited until her door closed before grabbing Tori's hand firmly.

Ignoring her squeal of protest, I held onto it until we reached my door at the end of the hall. Entering it, I pulled her over to the massive bed and sat her down on the plush mattress. "Sit."

She opened her mouth, no doubt to give me a blistering piece of her mind, but I placed one finger against her lips. "Please."

Not waiting for an answer, I turned back to the still-open door and closed it, turning the lock without hesitation. This was a rare moment with Tori alone and I was going to make sure nothing spoiled it.

Pulling a chair over to face the end of the bed where Tori was watching me through suspicious eyes, I sat down.

Taking a steadying breath, I began, "Tomorrow, we may receive information that takes away all the strain of the past week. Or, we'll find out that the road to returning to a normal life will be a bit bumpier than we hoped for. Either way, I want to start the day in the same manner I intend to end all the rest of my days."

She frowned. "In what way is that?"

"With you, by my side."

"Logan, I'm here. I told you I'm willing to give us a shot."

"And I think by saying that you allow yourself an easy way out."

"Out of what? It's not like we're twenty again and you've asked me to be your girlfriend," she scoffed.

"That's because we're in our thirties and I don't want you for my girlfriend, Tori."

Wincing, she grabbed a piece of the white coverlet, toying with it. "Then what exactly do you want from me, Logan?"

Leaning back, watching her closely, I replied. "I want you for my wife."

Chapter
Thirty-One

~

Tori

GASPING, MY HAND STILLED. I was locked into the bold invitation behind Logan's eyes after he dropped his bombshell declaration. Never in my most fantasy-filled dreams had I expected a proposal from the sublimely attractive man sitting in front of me, patiently waiting for a response. *Assuming that's what this is.*

"Is this a proposal?" I asked, stalling while my mind tried its best to make sense of what was happening.

"Not a proposal. Yet. More like a declaration of intent. I don't want there to be any doubts or misconceptions about what we're building toward, Tori. I can only hope you feel the same but if not, I think it's better to get it out in the open now."

He was doing it again. Leaving the ball in my court. It was a very effective maneuver, even I had to admit. It kept the fearmonger at bay, allowing me time to figure out if I wanted to take the next step.

This just happened to be a very large next step.

Searching his face for answers, I found something I wasn't used to seeing in Logan's features. Uncertainty. It was in the tense line of his jaw and the stillness of his frame. Knowing he was as unsure of my feelings as I had been about his helped knock my anxiety down a giant notch. Suddenly, it was as clear as he was sexy on how I intended to answer.

"Logan, you have to know by now that I'm in love with you. Even after I discovered your deception, I entrusted you with our lives. Sebastian worships you and I—well, despite the obvious anger at the current situation, I do care deeply for you. Otherwise, it wouldn't hurt this much."

I barely finished the last sentence before he gathered me into his arms. Only after I'd received a barrage of passionate kisses did I start squirming. He finally relented, pulling back to shine his joy into my eyes. "I love you, too. I think I fell for you the moment you walked into my office, Victoria McKinley. I've never met a woman who made me think of my future from the first glimpse of her. Not until you."

Amazed by the confession, I searched him for signs of exaggeration. Although he looked happy, he still looked like Logan. Calm, capable, and not about to lose his head in a moment.

Sighing, I rested my heated cheek on his shoulder, enjoying the feel of the cool cotton shirt. His arms tightened around me and I was filled with an almost overwhelming feeling of happiness.

Whatever came tomorrow, I knew I wouldn't be facing it alone.

I only hoped I wouldn't be asking my friends to endure whatever 'it' was along with me.

Chapter
Thirty-Two

~

Logan

CHECKING MY PHONE FOR the tenth time this morning, I quelled the urge to shout my frustration. Sitting in the living room waiting for Tori and Sebastian to put on their bathing suits, I was left with a plethora of energy and no outlet to dispose of it.

It was surprising, even to me, how much energy I had following last night. After Tori and I had made our feelings clear for each other, we spent hours talking, piecing together the portions of our lives that were previously unknown. Afterward, I had spent the night showing her body how much I worshipped it physically. As it had proven, we no longer had a trust issue. A satisfied grin tugged at one side at the memory.

Mrs. Lightwell walked by, a few towels in her hand.

"Excuse me, Mrs. Lightwell," I called out to her.

She stopped, startled. "I didn't see you there, sir. What can I do for you?"

"Are those towels for us?"

"Why yes, they are. I heard a group of you were heading out to the pool and I thought I'd make sure you had enough towels to go around."

"You're very thoughtful. I'm happy to take those off your hands. I'm going out now to check the water temperature before everyone jumps in. I was hoping you'd send word to Ms. McKinley that I'll meet them out there?"

She handed me the stack of towels, smiling easily. "Of course, sir. I'll send Summer to her. And thank you. Saves these aching feet of mine a trip, and with Mr. Ravenschall and all his guests arriving for lunch, I'm going to need them in tip-top shape."

Stopping my exit, I turned back to her. "Did you say Mr. Ravenschall and guests are arriving today?" I knew it was what she said but my mind didn't want to accept the news. I wasn't sure why he wouldn't have informed me directly. He had to know how important his news was to me. To all of us.

"Yes, sir. I'm sorry, I just assumed you knew! He's bringing Miss Ana and her beau, Mr. Justin's uncle, and another man he says is a friend of yours."

David? Why would he be coming unless the news was bad and a new plan needed to be discussed? That could also explain why my father hadn't called me with the news. He'd rather break it to me in person. Shit.

Sighing, I sent a reassuring smile to the housekeeper. "It must have slipped my mind that it was today. I won't hold you up any longer though. I'm sure you have a lot to prepare. Thanks again for the towels."

"It's no problem at all. Enjoy your swim, Mr. Logan." With that, she hurried out of the room.

A swim was exactly what I needed, and I reached the pool in minutes. Throwing the towels on a lounge chair, I kicked off my shoes while leaving on the simple white t-shirt I had worn in the house. Not bothering to check the temperature, I dove into the water.

***

"Well, that was the perfect way to spend a hot mid-morning," Tori purred, stretching out on the chair next to me.

"Although it was nice, I can think of a few other ways that would have made it even better."

"Only a few?"

"You'll have plenty of time to find out."

"Mmm."

I sent her a wink before checking on Sebastian. Nick and Summer were taking turns pulling him around the shallow end on a raft we found in the shed.

Tori followed my line of sight, smiling at her son's laughter. "He's having the time of his life here. I'm afraid home is going to seem very dull when this all blows over."

Guilt crashed over me. I hadn't told her what Mrs. Lightwell had revealed. It was too perfect a day to ruin with bad news yet. Checking my watch, I realized my father would likely be doing just that in the next hour or so. It was almost lunch time.

"He's a tough kid. I think he'll come out of this better than the rest of us."

Tori must have heard the despair in my voice because she turned to me sharply. I couldn't see her eyes behind the dark shades, but I could imagine the questioning look. "Is everything OK?"

"I'm not sure," I expelled, preparing myself for ruining our idyllic morning. "I found out this morning that—"

"Mr. Logan! Your father just arrived. They just got him and a few others he brought with him settled in their rooms. Lunch is being put out now." Steve interrupted, striding up to us with Pete at his heels. I didn't like the way Pete was looking at Tori in her sexy black suit and I sat up, blocking her from his view.

"Thank you, Steve. I'll be in momentarily." Nodding to him, I turned my attention back to Pete, daring him with a look to prolong his stay. He had the good sense finally to avert his eyes, following behind Steve without a single look back.

"Your father is here? I thought he was going to call you?" Tori asked, faint accusation in her tone.

"He was. I didn't find out until right before I came out here that plans had changed. I didn't want to ruin our morning by telling you, in case it meant bad news."

She grabbed my hand with one hand and removed her glasses with the other. Her hazel eyes looked stunning in the bright light as she answered, "We agreed we're a team now, remember? We face the good and the bad together. Got it?"

Love for Tori swelled as I pulled her in for a hard kiss. "Yes, my future," I breathed against her lips.

Her cheeks reddened but she squeezed my hand. "Let's go see what your father has to say." Louder, she said, "Sebastian, it's time to go inside and get ready for lunch."

Expecting protests, I realized we'd all worked up an appetite as he exited the pool without a fight. Summer and Nick joined us for the walk, until Nick parted ways at the back door with a lingering look for Summer.

Things are certainly progressing there, I thought with a smile.

Shivering as the cool air hits me, I raced Sebastian and Tori to the stairs before taking them two at a time.

We all disappeared in our rooms for several moments before meeting back in the hallway, fully clothed.

"I'm hungry!" Sebastian cried, rubbing his belly over his alien print t-shirt.

"Me too," I agreed. "I wonder what Mrs. Meetree has in store for us today?"

"Summer said today's menu is Italian-based, in honor of your father's preferences."

Tori looked good enough to eat in a Cajun-red halter dress that clung to her curves.

"Interesting. It seems the old man and I have quite a few things in common," I replied, already anticipating the coming meal. *Now, if only the meeting afterward would prove as satisfactory.*

Walking into the dining room, we stopped at the view of the overpacked room. Another table had been added and they'd been arranged into a triangle of sorts, allowing for easier conversation among the occupants.

My eyes immediately sought out Ana, who was smiling next to her blonde-haired boyfriend, Justin. Arthur was on one side of them while my father flanked Ana's other side. It was the fifth member of their table that had me doing a double take.

"Jax?" I called out into the busy room.

The volume of the room dipped as a few people turned to see who I was talking to.

Jax's face contorted into his version of a greeting.

"Surprised to see me?" he asked, clearly enjoying my discomfiture. "That's twice I've been able to shock you in recent months," he dug. "Guess it's a good thing you're retiring. Losing your edge, boy."

My father snorted. "He's a damn sight quicker than you are, you old wallybags. Almost had to get out the smelling salts when you first caught sight of us. You looked like you'd seen a ghost."

Jax grunted and I marveled at the sight of him sitting so comfortably at my father's table.

"They're a few seats here for you three," my father nodded to the large space between Jax at the beginning of his table and Jarrod, who made up the end of the adjoining one.

I could only nod, turning to guide Sebastian and Tori toward the food.

"Who's Jax?" Tori asked softly as we walked to the buffet tables.

"He's basically my superior. Remember I mentioned him when I told you about my start in this career?"

"Oh, wow! I remember now. He seems to know your father pretty well."

Looking back at the two of them laughing comfortably, I shook my head. "I've been as surprised by the revelation as you have. The two of them have a lot of questions to answer and I intend to get the answers today."

"I'd say you deserve them," she said, indignant on my behalf. It felt good to know there was someone to share these thoughts with now. Surreal, but good.

"And I'd say you better make sure you eat up, sweetheart. You're going to need your strength later," I whispered against her ear.

She shivered, her lips parting. Deliberately, I stepped back, turning toward Sebastian to ask which of the types of pasta he wanted to start with first. I was rewarded with a discreet pinch as Tori joined in our deliberations.

Focusing on the steaming chafing dishes, I prepared myself for an afternoon of shameless gluttony. Anything to keep my mind off the meeting to follow.

Chapter Thirty-Three

Tori

WATCHING THE TABLES CLEAR out slowly, I took a few minutes to reflect on how quickly things had progressed since Logan confessed his feelings.

We had shared childhood stories and dreams for our future, both delighting in the compatibility of our ideals. That rosy feeling had billowed out, swathing us in a blanket of desire. If I had harbored any doubts about his feelings before, his tender lovemaking afterward had taken care of them. I had never felt so cherished during the physical act. Before everything had exploded into a thousand pieces, he had commanded me to focus my eyes on him. The fact that he climaxed alongside me had made the entire experience seem cosmic, as if it were so much more than our bodies in perfect alignment.

To my delight, he had barely let the embers burn before reigniting the fire in us both. We had made clever use of several different spots in the master suite.

And then this morning, at the pool. Shaking my head, I considered the sight of him that had greeted me when Sebastian and I had arrived, sunglasses and sunscreen in hand. In fact, after receiving Logan's message from Summer and asking her to come along, I had almost regretted the invitation when I saw Logan rising from the tiled edge.

The scene played out in my head like a nineties romance movie. Strong arms, corded with muscles flexing underneath his glistening skin, had lifted his body out of the water. It was the sight of the chiseled chest and bulging abs showing through his paper-thin white shirt that had sent heat coursing through me. My mouth had gone slack at the slicked back hair dripping with water, its black appearance contrasting against his light olive skin. His green eyes had shone more vibrantly than I had ever seen them, the light reflecting from the water illuminating them.

Now I understood the appeal of wet t-shirt contests. There was something so enticing about a wet, fit body being revealed slowly through clinging fabric.

Although the physical side of things was moving along nicely, it was our emotional connection that saw the biggest improvement. I hadn't realized how much uncertainty was holding us both back from just enjoying one another. That is, until it had disappeared.

Gone were the barriers that kept us from showing our feelings for one another. Sebastian had picked up on it right away, giving Logan a spontaneous hug in the water. "You make mommy happy," he said simply.

Logan had returned his hug, looking up at me. "I want to make both of you happy, for as long as you'll both have me," he returned.

My eyes misted and I was busy blotting them when Nick had approached us, asking if we minded him joining us.

After a quick look at Summer's face, we had waved him in.

We'd made a merry party, playing pool games and swimming laps until our muscles protested. Logan and I had gotten out of the refreshing water to enjoy some rest before Steve walked up with his announcement.

It was Steve, now, that snapped me back to the present. "We've set the chairs in the library, as you requested Mr. Ravenschall."

"Excellent, Steve. Thank you. Gentlemen, Ms. McKinley, shall we?"

My breath hitched as I realized we were finally going to get the news we'd been both dreading and anticipating, depending on the hour. Looking over at Summer, I nodded toward Sebastian, tilting my head in silent question.

"Sebastian, your mom is going to be in a boring meeting. Do you want to come with Nick and me to watch Return of the Jedi?" She turned and asked him, taking my cue.

"Yes! Mom, can I go, please?"

"Of course, bud. Make sure you do as you're told though, got it?"

"Yes, momma! Thank you! Cool, let's go! Hey, do you guys have any popcorn?" His voice faded as they rounded the corner.

Summer looked back at me and waved.

'*Thank you,*' I mouthed right before she disappeared.

Following Logan into the hallway, I took in deep, slow breaths, trying to reduce the tightness in my chest.

As we entered the library, I looked around for an empty seat and was stopped by Logan's hand clasping mine.

"Whatever it is, we face it together," he said firmly. He found a pair of chairs next to the mini bar and we looked at each other, grinning.

"At least we're prepared for whatever comes," I laughed, some of the tension easing.

"I call the Johnnie Walker."

Wrinkling my nose, "Ugh, you've got it."

He chuckled, giving my hand a squeeze before releasing it.

I looked up, noting that Logan's father was standing in the middle of the informal arrangement of chairs. Ana, Justin, and Professor Cummings were in front of us, toward the right side of the room, while Jax and Jarrod were on the left.

Clearing his throat, Mr. Ravenschall began, "I'm sorry to have pulled you all from your daily activities, but what I have to say is of grave importance to us all."

That doesn't sound promising. Tiny beads of moisture gathered along my temples.

"As you know, Ana and Justin put themselves in the line of fire to help close a case that has baffled several of the brightest minds in the intelligence field for decades. It has taken us this long to narrow down a very lengthy list of organizations and individuals involved in a trafficking ring. After several dead ends, some stemming from the loss of our own brave officers, we finally got lucky. The information that Ana was able to retrieve provided the missing link that had confounded us all. We are organizing a sting the size of which will blow your minds. It will save thousands of lives from falling into the wrong hands. I've brought a man here to explain any of the questions you may have that I cannot answer. I shouldn't have to say this, but I want to stress the importance of keeping anything you hear in this room to yourselves. No one outside these walls needs to know the details of what we are about to discuss."

Satisfied with our confirmations, he gestured to Jax. "This is Jax and he works for the CIA. He's the man responsible for recruiting me and Logan's mother, Evelyn. He has also guarded two very precious assets of mine for the past two decades."

I felt the sudden tension in Logan beside me. Squeezing his knee in comfort, I was relieved when his hand covered mine.

Jax stood up, shaking Mr. Ravenschall's hand before turning to us. "A lot of these cases can be solved with meticulous surveillance, well-placed eyes and ears, and of course, following the money trails. What had eluded us for so long about this case was that the clients of these bastards often had impressive surveillance of their own. Every time we got close; a door shut. An asset was found dead, papers were shredded, a raided location said to be housing victims came up empty.

Eventually we wised up and stopped digging as hard at the suspected clientele. We focused on the supply channel, asking ourselves where the most vulnerable populations were. We realized they were likely those who were seeking asylum in our country. Scared, poor, alone, and forced to trust complete strangers with their lives. They were sitting targets. Slowly, we started infiltrating border protection units and embassies. One of our agents overheard a conversation at the U.S. Embassy and Consulates in Brazil that mentioned a shell company we had already flagged for suspicious activity." He paused, looking over at Logan. "You might remember the bastard who owned that business, Raven. Christoff Blanc."

"So, that's why he was being investigated?" Logan asked beside me.

"Yes, we didn't want him to think he could file for bankruptcy and disappear. We put every agency on his ass we could, citing him for everything from tax evasion to wire fraud. It was all a means to delay and distract him from knowing we were onto his darker operations. Thanks to his daughter, Mikaela, we ran out of time."

"How did she play into it?"

"She had been approached by the FBI, who were trying to flip her and get access to more of her father's private documents. I sent one of our guys to make sure she played nice because I knew from your previous reports that she wasn't likely to. It proved to be a costly mistake on my part. She seduced the poor bastard and he gave up your identity as a former participant in her father's investigation. She hoped to find out from you when we were going to move on her father so she could set herself up a little hidden nest egg."

"So that's where the leak in our agency came from. Who was it?" Logan asked, tight-lipped.

"I'm not sure you want—"

"Cut the shit. Who was it, Jax?" The anger emanating from Logan was like its own dark force. It was the first time I was glad to feel his hand leave mine.

"It was James Snyder."

The room was silent as we all watched the play of emotions on Logan's face. I glanced at Ana and she caught my eye, shaking her head gently. She was warning me to keep out of it and I complied unhappily, sitting still beside him.

"Shit," he burst out before slumping forward in his chair, his hands clutching his head so hard I was afraid he'd do himself damage.

Jax and Mr. Ravenschall both stepped forward and I slid to a seat a few feet away. This was something they needed to help him with, I understood instinctively. I'd be here to pick up the remaining pieces.

"Raven, you can't fault yourself. Snyder knew you were in pain the day he decided to be your sparring partner. He admitted as much to me. Said he was tired of watching you succeed at everything and thought you'd be distracted enough in your grief over Ana to take you down a notch. He got what he deserved, even though you never knew it until now," Jax patted Logan on the shoulder.

"You have to let go of the guilt, son, or it'll tear at your insides until you're just a shell. Trust me, I know."

At that, Logan looked up, locking eyes with his father. "Her death wasn't your fault, either. I think she always knew that lock of hair was mine, Dad. You can't keep blaming yourself for her decision."

His father's eyes gleamed. "Thank you, son. We'll talk about that another time. For now, I need to know you understand what Jax is saying. None of this was your fault."

Searching both men's faces a moment, Logan slowly nodded his head, straightening. He looked at the empty seat beside him before glancing up, catching my worried gaze. "Come here, Tori, please. I want you by my side."

As I complied, he leaned forward to kiss my temple. "Always," he whispered.

I caught the light of approval in Mr. Ravenschall's eyes as he and Jax backed away, turning to stand before the room again.

"Until we have apprehended everyone, we are still on high alert. However, it won't be long until life resumes some normalcy. Logan, Tori, we will keep the detail on the Pratt's and the Marquez's until further notice. We've let them know that a conclusion to all this is near. Oh, and Mrs. Marquez asked me to relay a message to you, Logan. She said, 'Tell him I knew I wasn't wrong, but he still has some explaining to do'."

Logan snorted and I hid a smile. That was Cami's version of telling him she forgave him. Mostly.

Mr. Ravenschall continued, "David and Liz are holed up at an undisclosed location, and Ana, Justin, and Mr. Cummings will all be placed together in a different safehouse. I'll keep you briefed daily," Logan's father nodded, dismissing the room.

Jax approached me, the slight tilt of his scraggly mouth attempting a smile. "It's a pleasure to meet you, Ms. McKinley. I have heard a lot about you over the past couple of months. Hopefully, you'll keep this hard head out of trouble in retirement."

Logan jerked beside me, reaching out to grasp Jax's forearm. "Does that mean...?"

"I already filed the paperwork. You're a free man, Raven. Logan," he corrected himself gruffly. "We're losing one of the best. It's been a pleasure all these years. Take care of yourself. Take care of them." He returned Logan's arm grasp and then turned abruptly to Ana. "I'll see you soon."

"Looking forward to it," she winked audaciously.

"You Ravenschall's will be the death of me," he grumbled, saluting to Mr. Ravenschall as he turned to walk out the room.

Ana introduced me to Justin, and I found him to be as charming as she was. It was the man standing slightly behind him that I was most interested in, though.

As Logan conversed with Justin and Ana, I greeted the blustery giant. "Hello, Professor Cummings," I smiled up at him, holding out my hand.

The reddening of his cheeks was barely perceptible through his facial hair, but I knew his dear face well. "Hello Ms. McKinley. I'm sure you want to rake me over the coals for getting you involved in all this," he said in his gravelly voice, ducking his head.

"Actually, I wanted to give you this," I replied, standing on my tiptoes and throwing my arms around the giant man. Kissing his coarse cheek, I pulled back in time to see moisture gathering in his eyes before he wiped them quickly and patted my head awkwardly. "Thank you, Professor Cummings. You gave me a gift I can never hope to repay you for."

"You can start by calling me Arthur," he said hoarsely. "It seems only fitting since we may be related one day." He looked over at Justin and Ana, who were laughing with Logan. "If my grandson ever gets his head out his a—" he stopped.

Laughing, I looked back at the couple, noting how Justin stayed close by Ana no matter where she moved. "I don't think you'll have to worry about that for long."

His face softened. "No, no I don't believe I will." He leaned in, "And I don't think you'll have long to wait, either, young lady."

"Logan, Tori, I need to speak to both of you. Alone, please. Follow me," Mr. Ravenschall boomed across the room, standing by the door that led outside.

Looking to Logan, I searched for clues as to why we were being summoned. His face was filled with similar curiosity. He joined us, shaking Arthur's hand before taking mine.

"Let's see what the man full of enigma has to surprise us with now, shall we?"

Chapter
Thirty-Four

~

Logan

LEADING TORI OUT THE library doors and into the yard, I wondered what my father had left up his sleeve. The revelations made within the past several days had been enough to knock my entire world off-kilter. If I hadn't had the woman next to me, I doubted I'd ever have found my axis again. She and Sebastian anchored me, filling me with a purpose I never knew I was lacking.

My father stopped in front of a giant structure—shed, from the look of it. Mr. Brander's mention of a workshop came to mind and as my father swung open the door, I realized I was right.

Only, it was no ordinary workshop. I recognized the woodworking tools spaced out along the concrete floor of the building. Similar machines had been in my former woodshop teacher's shop, although there were a couple unfamiliar ones here, too.

"I had no idea you were into woodworking, Dad," I told him in awe. "It must have taken a while to collect all of these."

"It did. I had some help from a friend of yours though," he said, a sparkle in his eyes.

"So, it *was* you who arranged all that?" I asked, although I'd worked out most of it in my head.

"Yes. Your mother shared your interests with me as often as she could over the years. When it was time for you to strike out on your own, I wanted to do what I could to help, even from afar. So, I sent Jax to offer you one way of life and Barry to offer you another. You ended up choosing both, which I didn't anticipate," he laughed. "But I figure now you'll have some extra time on your hands, you'll need these tools to make effective use of it."

"I'm flattered that you'd house them at your property, but—"

"Not my property, Logan," he said evenly. "Yours."

I heard Tori's gasp next to me before it was replaced by a loud ringing in my head. Looking around for a place to sit, I was grateful as my father pulled out a stool and helped me onto it.

"Woah, steady, my boy. I know you've had a lot of shocks lately But I'm hoping this is a good one."

I could only stare at the man who had turned out to be so much more than I could ever have hoped for. He had been forced to watch his children from the sidelines but had been with us every step of the way. The emotions the realization brought overcame my control and I lunged for my father, enveloping him in all the pent-up love I had never had the chance to show him.

"Thank you, Dad," I whispered against his shoulder, not caring that I had soaked it. An overwhelming flood of regret for our past mixed with appreciation for the promise of our future.

"You betcha, son. You didn't think I'd leave you to fend for yourself after all these years, did you?" he asked, pulling back. Wiping underneath both eyes, he cleared his throat. "I am also hoping I can convince you to start learning the business. If you just want to begin with the consulting side you originally planned to get into, I'm fine with that. I work with a lot of different clients and I'm sure we can find some that appeal to you that will benefit from your expertise. What do you say?"

Looking over at Tori, I answered, "That depends on the benefits. How's your family plan?"

Her face crumbled tears streaming down her silken cheeks. I reached her in two steps. "Shh, sweetheart. It's alright. Whatever it is, we'll fix it," I soothed, gathering her against me, anxious to make the smile return to her lips.

My father stepped beside me, holding out a small black box. Putting his finger to his lips, he mouthed, 'Your mothers' before winking and leaving us alone.

Opening the box carefully, I was in awe of the large emerald ring twinkling from the satin enclosure.

Tori squirmed in my arms. "I'm not upset," she got out, a radiant smile forming, "I'm happier than I've ever been in my life. I love you, Professor Mitch Logan 'Raven' Ravenschall," she laughed against my lips as I leaned in to taste her.

Pulling back to kneel in front of her, I held out the open box.

"And I adore you, Miss Victoria 'Tori' McKinley Ravenschall-to-be. I can't wait to spend eternity showing you just how much."

Author's Note

I hope you enjoyed the story of how Tori broke her losing streak with love and Logan found a woman to love the man behind the façade.

Now that they have sorted (most) things out, it is time to follow along with David and Liz to see if they can overcome the wounds of the past. Look for their story in the third installment of the Emerald Raven series in the spring of 2022.

Whatever your own HEA looks like, may you find it (or it find you) in good faith and health, and with a fighting spirit.

As always, I welcome your reviews or comments about the story.

~~~

Thank you for your support!

Rose

Acknowledgments

———— ～ ————

Thank you to my editor, Nikki Boccelli-Saltsman, for your professional guidance and wisdom. To my cover artist, Angie with Pro_ebookcovers, for the lovely artwork. And as always, my sincere appreciation to Will Silva for the attractive interior formatting.

I've met some wonderful members of the writing and reading communities, and to them I give my most humble thanks. You motivate and inspire me to continue meandering along this challenging but rewarding path.

About the Author

Rose Walken is a U.S. romantic fiction author. When she isn't writing or spending time with her children, brother-sister pair of rescue cats, and fiancé, you can find her gardening, crafting, or researching various oddities.

She loves to hear from her fans and welcomes you to sign up to receive notifications of new releases, giveaways, blog postings, and other important updates. Visit her on the web at www.rosewalken.com and subscribe today!